To Bea

BY

MEGAN WRIGHT

PublishAmerica

Baltimore

First printing

ISBN: 1-4137-1143-X
PUBLISHED BY PUBLISHAMERICA, LLLP
www.publishamerica.com
Baltimore

Printed in the United States of America

To Mom

WHO SHINES LIKE A GEM
IN A FIVE AND DIME STORE.

"A ship in port is safe but that's not what ships are for. Sail out to sea and do new things."

—REAR ADMIRAL GRACE HOPPER

Chapter One

It wasn't smooth sailing in the office today. The abrupt drone of the dial tone signaled yet another rejection.

"Hello. How are you today? I'd like to tell you about..."

Click.

"Hello. Have you heard about...?"

Click.

"Hello. How are you?"

"I'm fine."

"That's good. I just want to take a minute to tell you about..."

Click.

"Hello. How are you today? I'm here to tell you about...

"Oh, I'm glad you called," he responded. "I'm selling life insurance. I'm curious...do you have full coverage?"

Click.

Is THAT what we sound like?

My name is Bea. Bea is short for Beatrice. I am also short on patience these days. I am a telemarketer. I don't need to sell people on the idea of Michigan. I know that it is beautiful. What I'm trying to sell is travel discounts. You know...if one person visits the cherry festival for ten dollars a second person attends free.

People feel as if they have every right to be unkind and read the riot act to me. At some point in time, people decided that it was okay to snipe at people in service industries, clerks, and especially at telemarketers.

I admit that sometimes some phone solicitors call near dinnertime or some don't take no for an answer. I'm not proud of that kind of behavior. More often than not, however, telemarketers are like me and are barely making a minimum wage. Often we are calling with a genuinely good deal. Those facts don't stop the people who answer from being unkind. They could simply say they aren't interested and please don't call again.

Instead, so many people are angry with telemarketers. People preach tolerance for every living thing but the majority seems to think that it's okay to be unkind to a phone solicitor. I find myself in one of the least popular jobs of our times!

Some telemarketers grow used to it. The same way a bare foot develops calluses over the summer for protection, a telemarketer can develop a thicker skin when making calls.

I never quite developed that thick skin. But I am also reaching the sixth month anniversary of my job and that's right about when I start getting antsy at every job I've had so far.

I have had several jobs during my somewhat cloistered adulthood. I worked in retail as a managerial trainee. That job kept me at the store until 12:30 one night because the floors needed cleaning. I was nervous about those late hours alone in the store. A kind employee, who worked that evening, volunteered to stay with me so I wouldn't be afraid. As I was closing the store an alarm went off. I jumped, searched the store and found that a door was ajar. It was okay. There was no problem after all. I wished my heart would stop its ferocious pounding. The danger was over. I lasted at my retail job until the end of my training. By that point in time, I knew it wasn't the life for me.

I also have worked in publishing. It was the best of times and it was the worst of times. The people at the company were wonderfully friendly and bright. Most people had a good sense of humor. The company didn't pay its employees much money.

Someone in management put up a sign about the arrival of cookie orders that read "Girl Scout cookies will be distributed on the ninth floor."

An impoverished employee wrote on top of the sign so it now read, "In lieu of pay, Girl Scout cookies will be distributed on the ninth floor."

The publishing company amassed a good group of workers, but the pay was abysmal. Since everyone there was bright, promotions often came as a result of attrition. Most people were capable of doing more creative work than what the reference book company asked them to do.

Some employees were wonderfully loyal. They knew that no other company in the area would treat them—the ones with non-technical degrees—this well.

I loved my co-workers but I disliked my job. I had to proofread a computer-generated index. It was dull. Plus, my bus commute was a 45-minute express in the morning at 6 a.m. and a 1½ hour trip in the afternoon, at 3:20 p.m.

I lasted at the job four years. That was a record for me. But I had to move on.

At the time, moving on meant that I went back to school and got another degree. I taught kindergarten for one year, part time. Once again a small salary followed me but that was the least of my worries. I couldn't get the children to listen to me. Not being a mom, I never developed the mother's stare that showed I meant business. I cried my last day of school and so did some of my students. They cried because it was the end of a fun year. I cried because I knew it was the end of my teaching career. I simply couldn't get the kids under control and that is perhaps one of the most important lessons a kindergarten teacher can learn.

I have been a legal secretary for an unsavory group of lawyers. I am predisposed to like lawyers because my dad was an attorney. But, to show the true colors of my employers, one of them put a post-it note on the back of one of the young and naïve secretaries that read, "Screw me" only in more explicit language. The poor woman wore it all around the office, oblivious that a so-called professional would demean her like that. You would think a lawyer would be brighter than that. And people get mad at telemarketers! If they only knew!

I also worked as a store clerk at an office supply store. The bad part was I saw a lot of my successful high school friends come in and shop as I had the less-than-prestigious job standing behind the cash register. The nice part was I ran into some old high school friends who were pretty nice. Eventually I became restless there also. Time to move on.

At one point I worked with a good friend as a housecleaner. Our training involved going out with experienced housecleaners. The experienced cleaners called smoking a cigarette choking down a bone. It was like a whole new world to me. Up until that point my jobs were non-manual. This, by contrast, was physical labor. And while there is nothing wrong with an honest day's work, my friend quit cleaning houses and it wasn't any fun without her. The worst part of cleaning houses was when the homeowners were there, watching you, hovering about you and telling you all the spots you missed.

I also worked in a condemned factory putting old files in new boxes to be placed in the new building for future use. As bad as it sounds, and it really was a condemned factory, this was where that I learned to play Euchre. My bosses were wonderfully nice and insisted that we workers take breaks now and then. As grimy as the job was, the bosses were among the best I've ever had.

Postmistress and camp counselor are also on my resume. These were summer jobs. They were perhaps my happiest work experiences. Summer and happy used to be synonymous with me.

I have seen a large spectrum of the work world. Holding a lot of different jobs is one thing. Fitting into the work world is altogether different. I never quite mastered that.

Chapter Two

My persistent restlessness must come from my great Uncle Ned. He worked on the freighters in the Great Lakes. He was never at a port too long but he had an exciting life and he always has lots of stories to tell. Working on a freighter didn't mean dealing with the public the way being a telemarketer did. It meant seeing stunning sights around Michigan.

I am close to my great Uncle Ned and have actively kept in touch with him. He reciprocates. Uncle Ned tells me that his first Christmas card of the year is always from me. And he is right. I write my Christmas cards Thanksgiving evening. Maybe I rush things a bit but I can't wait to get in touch with all the people I love.

Great Uncle Ned surprised me with an unbelievable gift. He was always kind about giving me a check for fifteen dollars as a present. Instead, this time, he handed me an envelope. It said, "To Bea."

Inside was a note that read:

> "If you seek a pleasant peninsula, look about you." That's Michigan's state motto. It's also true. Go and see for yourself!
> Love,
> Uncle Ned

Uncle Ned had given me a ticket to cruise the Great Lakes. He wasn't a wealthy man. From outward appearances he wasn't a sentimental man. He is kind to me and incredibly sweet. He wanted me to see what he had seen while working on the freighters. Uncle Ned wanted me to experience the Great Lakes by the best way possible—by boat. He splurged on me and I am grateful beyond words! Uncle Ned wanted me to have this gift while he was still alive so we could swap stories.

"If you seek a pleasant peninsula, look about you." I was so excited to think that I was actually about to do that.

A peninsula is a body of land surrounded by water on three sides. Michigan has two peninsulas, the upper and the lower.

I had heard of these cruises. Some can be more expensive than crossing the Atlantic on the QE2. Great Uncle Ned saved up enough so that I could do it in style.

My great-great uncle, Uncle Ned's father, was the first one to make his home in southeast Michigan. Soon, the rest of the family followed. Everyone trusted Ned Senior's knack for finding nice places to live. He had discovered the best hunting spot in Maine.

His home on the Indian River in Florida was wonderful. Where Ned led, people followed.

Thus family followed when Ned Senior moved to Michigan. My Uncle Ned, Ned Jr., made the decision to work on the freighters in the Great Lakes. He was about 15 his first summer on the lakes and he loved it. He told me he became strong and muscular. He also told me how he grew up emotionally because of being away from home and not being coddled by his mother. His boss didn't care if he felt homesick or seasick. Uncle Ned had a job to do and that was that.

His first time on a freighter started at Lake Michigan near Chicago and went up past Superior, through the Straits of Mackinac (pronounced Mac—in—aw) to Lake Huron, Lake Erie, and Lake Ontario. Then the freighter plodded on along to transport tons of goods through the St. Lawrence Seaway. It was the biggest thrill of his life. Just because he was on fresh water didn't mean the weather was always mild. Uncle Ned had to endure one storm on Lake Erie in particular on his first voyage.

It was a thunderstorm that hit in the middle of the night. Uncle Ned told how he could hear the rumble of thunder in the background and as it grew closer it became louder. It wasn't long before he heard and saw the crackle of lightning. The sky lit up like a Fourth of July fireworks display. That got his attention! Water swept over the deck of the freighter, immediately, the captain told everyone to put on a lifejacket. Everyone on deck had to secure his clip to a line connected to the boat so as not to be swept overboard. Uncle Ned feared for his life. Would they all drown? Would a big wave snap the freighter in two? It had happened to others! Ned didn't know the exact number of ships that lost their battle with the Great Lakes but plenty more than made Ned comfortable.

The rain kept coming down harder and harder. A light in the distance flashed on and off. It turned out to be a lighthouse. Another light on the lake probably meant a boat was nearby. Uncle Ned wondered if his boat was in danger. He also wondered if the boat near him posed a threat.

Then, suddenly, another crash of thunder sounded loudly, the lightning made it bright as day and then the winds picked up.

Ned was scared to death!

A brief silence and then there was another steady stream of rain and slight thunder. The rain stayed with the boat. It grew louder. The raindrops were large. The captain said he'd try to get them to a safe cove. Uncle Ned wondered: would the freighter make it? Could the captain navigate through this storm? Or would they all wind up as debris on the shoreline?

After what seemed like an interminable night, the dawn started to emerge. The thunder stopped. The rain stopped. For a brief moment Ned thought his heart had stopped. He had never been through anything like that before.

Uncle Ned told me that since Erie is the shallowest of the Great Lakes, the winds pick up faster there and can create not a wave but a wall of water that would frighten even a seasoned seafarer. This was his first big storm on the water. He told me he found religion that night. He also said he never felt so alive.

Uncle Ned told me that storm on Erie was a turning point for him. He would continue this work for as long as he was able. He was able for years. The new recruits turned to Ned for advice and for courage during storms. They figured if Old Ned was still around, these boats must be capable of handling whatever the Great Lakes threw at them.

Uncle Ned has taken me aside ever since I was a little girl and he keeps saying that Michigan is a very special state because it is surrounded by water. He says that there is something spiritual in being surround by three-quarters of the planet's surface water. Ned told me that he wasn't alone in his beliefs. Uncle Ned explained that the Native Americans gave Michigan its name "michi" and "gama" meaning "big lake." He told stories of how Native Americans around the Great Lakes believed in Winabojo who was the ruler of all human, animal and plant life.

Ned wasn't a churchgoer but he knew nature could humble man in an instant and he believed a Greater Being controlled nature. He believed in God.

Uncle Ned felt closer to God when he was on the waterways then at any other time. He would ask, "How could you not believe in God when you see all the beauty around you? The Great Lakes are among His finest masterpieces."

My uncle doesn't confuse lying with politeness. He calls it as he sees it. The people Ned loved knew Ned loved them. He didn't have to waste a lot of extra words or send fancy cards. When Ned loved someone he gave something quite valuable…his time and his undivided attention.

To some people his sincere attention was the most precious gift offered. To some other people it didn't mean much at all. Uncle Ned never held that against anyone. He just liked to know the character of the people with whom he dealt. If his extra time was extra special, Ned could be wonderfully loyal and reliable. I love each and every moment Uncle Ned spends with me.

You know, I look at this ticket for my voyage and I almost want to cry. I can't believe how lucky I am that Uncle Ned wants to share his good times on the Great Lakes with me. The date for my excursion is very soon, in early fall. I will leave from Toronto and travel across all five of the Great Lakes. The trip will take seven nights from Toronto to Port Huron. The first night we would spend overnight on land in Toronto, Ontario. The next day we would board the ship. From there we would be off to the Welland Canal/Niagara Falls, Ontario and that involved crossing Lake Ontario. The third day was to be spent at sea traveling across Lake Erie and winding up in Port Huron, Michigan. Following that we would travel Lake Huron to Little Current, Ontario. Next stop, our fifth day, would be to the Soo Locks and cruising Lake Superior. From there we would go to Mackinac Island, Michigan and then cruise on Lake Michigan. On the last day we would arrive at Port Huron, our final destination.

If I stop to think about it I'm feeling a lot of different emotions all at once. I'm excited. I'm nervous. I'm thrilled. I'm petrified! Most people don't know this but I'm also a little bit shy. I like other people and I like to be polite but sometimes encountering new faces and new places can be painful. I know Uncle Ned certainly didn't want to put me on the spot. Yet in some odd sort of way he was doing me a big favor by forcing me to socialize. Think about it, I'm stuck on a boat. I don't want to be so shy that I'm also stuck in my cabin. I want to see the sights. I know most people are nice. I know the world is a better place than the news would have you believe. But I still get nervous in new situations. Good old Uncle Ned was teaching me more than one of life's lessons.

Ned's philosophy was that it is better to show love while one is still alive rather than have it be a total surprise at one's funeral. He also prefers to make the other person look good rather than being in the spotlight for himself. He excels at showcasing others. He is sweet to me and teases me in a way that I know he feels warmly toward me. I love it. I love him. Uncle Ned has charm and makes me feel special.

Am I excited about the trip? How could I not be? Of course I'm excited. I haven't been outside my state in a very long time. Now, all of a sudden, I will travel quite a bit. My first destination is Toronto.

I'm not really sure what to pack. Uncle Ned talked about the gorgeous scenes he witnessed as a crewmember on a freighter. One thing I know for certain is that I will pack a camera and a lot of film.

Should I pack an evening dress? I knew that during the time of paddleboats it was very popular to cruise the Great Lakes. I heard that at one point in history more people were asleep aboard vessels in the Great Lakes than in all of the oceans. That's pretty amazing. Cruising the Great Lakes seems to have gone the way of the train and yet, here and now these cruises are making a comeback.

Thinking of the old paddleboats and old fashioned passenger ships conjured up a picture of a large and ornate parlor inside the boat filled with cigar-smoking men playing poker and ladies in long dresses and big hats.

I can hear the tinny sound of an upright piano in the background. A bar would serve the men drinks. Ladies didn't drink. Some women might, though. I figure back then the word "lady" meant being refined and proper. Today the word "lady" could be preceded with the word "Hey" and mean total disrespect.

I am glad a lot of the strict code of conduct of a past era has melted away. "Women," "ladies," "girls," the words don't matter. What is nice about today is that a woman can pretty much follow her heart and her dreams more than ever before. Female doctors and lawyers, artists and poets no longer stand out as rarities. Women before me pioneered equality for women. I'm grateful. My mother had to work to establish credit. My problem today is not to be tempted to spend too much on a credit card.

Still, I don't think women are better than men. I think we should enjoy the same rights but in some ways we are different. Don't get me wrong...women can do anything they sets their minds to do. Men can do nearly anything too. I'm just stating the obvious that the politically correct have robbed from us—most women and men are different. In fact, no two people are alike, regardless of sex. I've never thought men are better than women. We all have intrinsic worth just by being human. Some people are nicer and smarter but it has nothing to do with their gender.

I hate the idea of a battle of the sexes. I do, however, love the opportunities everyone has today that we didn't always have. I might be a telemarketer, but I could be a rocket scientist if I had the inclination and the talent. I don't. I don't care for numbers and I'm not blessed with brilliance. But that has nothing to do with me being a woman.

Hey I've got to slow down. I was just wondering what to pack. I just know what I like and what I don't. What I like is that I'll soon be setting off on this great adventure.

Chapter Three

I read in the cruise's flyer that casual was the dress code. And yet, bathing suits were not allowed in public rooms. It sounds as if they are trying to keep a light atmosphere but still retain a sense of decorum. The brochure stated that the last night of the cruise was to be a costume party. "Bring a costume to wear to dinner the final night." The flyer also says that during the captain's welcome party the first night on board, the attire would be semi-formal.

Those few instructions set the tone. I had to think of a great costume. Other than that, I would pick my style to be casual preppy. I loved that look while I was in college although I never really did master it.

How hard can it be?

I'm not rich but I want every aspect of the voyage to be smooth sailing so I went online and looked up various catalogues. A flattering wrap dress from one place and a beautiful Norwegian sweater from another place and a pair of pleated khakis will all be perfect for this cruise. No stiletto heels for me. I'm headed for the wilderness.

These items are expensive but I've saved up a little and this is a trip of a lifetime. I don't think too many people actually care what I wear on the cruise but I'm shopping carefully anyway. I want to feel as if I fit it. This is just a simple way to start. At least I won't be packing a fur coat only to discover I'm on a cruise with animal activists! Don't laugh. It happens!

I have yet to master the art of packing lightly. I must prepare for all types of weather, warm, cold, rain, and sleet.... Having lived in Michigan my whole life, I am familiar with the saying that if you don't like Michigan's weather then just wait 15 minutes and it will change. In Michigan you don't simply pack for fall. You prepare for anything. In addition to my parka, I'm throwing in a pair of shorts, just to be safe.

It would be coldest on Lake Superior. Around Superior is something like 60 degrees in the summer. It's the deepest of the Great Lakes and the furthest north. Perhaps it is also the most beautiful. I read that Lake Superior is so clean that you can actually drink from the lake.

It makes me think of Hiawatha by the shores of Gitchi Gumi (Lake Superior). I can see myself as a young, Native American woman. I am wearing a doeskin dress. Around my neck I have strands of small beads, some made from shells. As I kneel beside the water, I cup my hands and drink. The crystal blue water is so pure that I am instantly refreshed.

"Bea!"

"Huh?"

"What were you doing? I've been calling you for five minutes now."

"I'm sorry Mom, I was just thinking about my trip. What do you want?" *She caught me in the middle of my daydream.*

I think my mom is great. She was born with the dramatic name Katrina Bouvella and she married my dad, Egbert. I guess I'm lucky that I got the name Bea. It could be much worse.

Mom gets along well with just about everyone. She doesn't have to be the center of attention. She is happy to sit back and let others brag. She realizes that it's much easier to get a point across if you have the other person making the point. The trick is getting him to see your point of view while he thinks it is his own.

She became somewhat adept at this early on.

My mom, who goes by the name Kat, would find a way to get Dad to tell her that he insists upon giving me some money for the trip. Thank God for Mom's arsenal.

She is not manipulative; she gently nudges people in the direction where they are ultimately headed. She is smart enough and group-minded enough to realize what is best in most situations. She also has faith in human nature. She says it pays to be nice. She claims everyone has some good in him. She takes the time to look for it. She claims that's why the mean people stand out from the crowd. I may not have as much faith in mankind as my mother does but the way she lives her life is an example that while life can be hard, it also can be fun! She prefers to focus on the positive. It's not that she sees the world through rose-colored glasses. Sure, she gets angry sometimes. But basically people seek her out for her upbeat personality.

"Bea," started Mom. "I was just going to say this should be a lot of fun for you."

"I can hardly wait. The fall colors should be gorgeous. Who all do you think would take a trip like this?" I asked.

Kat was in the kitchen, starting dinner. "I'll bet there are a lot of interesting people. I'm sure plenty of people will be from Michigan. Then again, it's a unique tour. You might meet all sorts of people from all sorts of places. I read that some Europeans take this cruise. In fact they instigated this new interest in cruising the Great Lakes. It's not just a local thing."

"What do you think the cruise will be like?" I wondered.

"I can't say for sure but I realize you're excited and nervous. Don't be nervous. But go ahead and get as excited as you want. This is no ordinary trip. Your Uncle Ned is just as keyed up about your trip as you are. He can hardly wait to hear what you think of the Great Lakes. He wants to compare notes with you." Kat just finished chopping the vegetables for chicken stir-fry.

"I'm nervous, Mom. Sure it'll be an adventure. But I'm not one to try something new just because it is new. And yet, part of this trip is already inside me because of all of Uncle Ned's stories. This is the calm before the storm. Once I set foot on the boat, I'm committed. I just want to be sure I can find a way to have fun without the jitters getting in the way. And despite all my whining, I can hardly wait for my adventure to begin. I've never been to Toronto before. Going there alone would be cool. Even the train ride to Toronto will be a special trip." As I spoke, I paced around the kitchen like a little kid who had too much sugar.

"How is your packing coming along?" Kat asked.

"I'm trying to cover all the bases. Do you think they'll let me take a steamer trunk?"

"I think that's a bit much for a seven-night trip." Kat laughed as she got out the soy sauce. "How many more days until your trip?"

"Two" I held up two fingers. "I have just enough time to get everything done."

"It sounds like you have already started your adventure."

Chapter Four

I flipped through a magazine on the train to Toronto. I couldn't believe I was guilty of half of the fashion don'ts. That's okay. Fashion goes out on a limb to be different. They keep changing the style to sell more clothes. I'm content with my outfits for the trip and so what if I'm not a model. At least I digest my food.

The train pulled into the station at Toronto. As I find my way to the hotel my heart is pounding. The escapades are beginning.

A nice man held the elevator for me on the way up to my room. Usually people don't talk in elevators. He did.

"You look happy." He grinned as he spoke. He looked happy too.

"You can't imagine," I burst forth.

"I see we're on the same floor. My name is James."

"Nice to meet you."

"So what's your secret? Why are you absolutely beaming?" James asked.

"I'm about to see all the Great Lakes. I've never done anything like this before. I'm getting excited just talking about it."

The elevator let us off at the appointed floor.

"Well, what do you know? I'll be on your ship. When I read about this trip I knew I had to take this cruise. I thought about making this a working vacation but I'm starting to think it's time to just unwind and enjoy myself." James was not too short and not too tall. He was pleasant to look at. He wasn't skinny but he didn't have an ounce of fat on him. I was trying to guess his age. I'm going to guess that he and I are close to the same age.

"What do you do?" I asked.

"I'm a photographer. I mostly take pictures of the outdoors."

"Then this trip is perfect for you. If it were me I would be snapping photos every two seconds. How do you know what makes a really good picture?"

Before he could answer I continued, "September in northern Michigan is about as pretty as it gets. It's hard to pick a favorite season in Michigan but I think the fall colors will make this trip spectacular." We stepped off the elevator together.

"Good company on the boat won't hurt this vacation either."

I hoped he meant he felt I was the good company he mentioned. No matter what he meant I had to agree with him...I also hoped the boat had lots of nice people. If not that then I hoped I'd get to spend a lot of time with James because he seems carefree and outgoing.

I looked at James more closely this time. He was handsome but not gorgeous. Thank God! First, I make it a policy never to date a man prettier than I am. Second, I find gorgeous men to be spoiled. James seems like a kind man and a gentle man. He seems confident and fun. He also seems smooth but not slick. He's definitely noteworthy.

"Gracious company is always a welcome sight—especially for travelers. I guess that's why I am so fond of the South," whispered a thin voice. Lydia Lane was from the South. She had a slight accent.

"You might find this hard to believe, so perhaps I shouldn't tell you, but I can be quite psychic. Here let me show you. I'd say you two have been married for about 15 years," Lydia predicted. Lydia didn't look like any of the psychics who advertise on TV.

James and I looked at each other. James smiled. I laughed.

"No, we just met." We chimed in unison.

"Well then I sense that you are about to part ways very soon," Lydia spoke again.

"No," James informed her. "We just found out we are going to be on the same cruise on the Great Lakes together."

"Well I should have known why I felt so much energy from you two. I'm going on that cruise myself." Lydia didn't give up.

"It should be fun. My name is Bea and this is James."

"I am Lydia. It's an easy name to remember. Just think of all the stories 'Lydia the Tattooed Lady' has. I have more!"

James asked both Lydia and me if we'd like to meet him at the hotel bar for a drink this evening. I said, "Sure" hoping this start to my adventure would begin smoothly. Lydia exuded charm as she accepted the "honorable invitation."

I thought she was laying it on a little thick but she seemed sweet enough and sincere enough. Who am I to judge?

All of a sudden we all heard a door slam.

"What was that all about?" I asked.

"I sense that college kids are acting like...well college kids. It's probably part of some prank," Lydia intuited.

With that one door opened and an older woman with bright red hair walked out of her room. She was wearing Capri pants with a matching top and looked confident without looking smug. Only the gray roots betrayed her age.

Then another door opened. It was next door to the redhead's room. Out came a small woman with blonde hair. She looked upset. She looked ageless. I thought of the woman in Shangri La. She was slim and peppy with no gray roots showing. She walked quickly and with grace.

The redhead said she was going to the lobby to look for a newspaper.

The smaller woman slammed her door once more.

"I don't think that they are college kids," James smirked.

James, Lydia and I all giggled. Then I thought, *Note to self: Lydia's psychic abilities stink.*

How going to the lobby can be grounds for a fight was beyond me. I realized that if real college kids had slammed the doors as loudly as they did that they would be the first to issue a complaint.

"I wonder if they'll be on our trip as well," pondered Lydia.

"Oh I'm sure they will be. I'm willing to bet a lot of people from this hotel, or at least from this floor of our hotel, are headed for our cruise." When James spoke you had confidence that what he was saying was accurate.

I was anxious to get settled in my room before heading off for a drink.

Unlike the women we just saw, I'm not ageless. Yet no age is limited by chronology. It's all your point of view. Now they say that if you live to the year 2010 you have a good chance of living to the ripe old age of 125. That would make middle age 62 ½. I'm just getting started.

No need to fret about trivial mistakes. That's for middle school kids. I guess worse than making a mistake or diving in is being too afraid to try. Now that's more of my issue. Meeting new people for drinks might sound like a piece of cake to most people. To me it is something of a challenge and today I accept that challenge.

I vow this trip to deal with my shyness. I'll also try to avoid getting so frustrated that I give up. Hey, wait a minute... isn't that the whole point of relaxing, not making big vows? If I plan to enjoy myself I need to relax. Easy for some but not for me!

I know I'm naïve. I know I've led a sheltered life. It's hard work being shy. I have to keep telling myself: *just get out there and experience life!* Some ventures will be better than others. That's the way it goes!

Good God, how did I get on that line of thought? I'm very happy right now. I'm headed for a thrilling ride and so far the people seem approachable. Seeing the good in life and meeting new friends are not mutually exclusive goals.

James wanted to go to his room before we would meet to have that drink. As he left, Lydia followed me and remarked, "That James fellow is handsome."

"Yes, I think so too."

"Did he say he was traveling with his wife?" Lydia asked.

"He didn't say but I think it's just him," I replied. I thought to myself that here I had met a nice man and some polished woman with the charm of the South comes along. I'm a daydreamer. She's a doer. I'm awkward. She's sophisticated. Well, at least James is nice, I told myself. Isn't that what this trip is about? There is no point in comparing myself to Lydia because we are two entirely different people. It's like comparing apples to...think, think, an exotic fruit...mangos!

Lydia stopped to look in a mirror in the hall of the hotel before we met James in the lounge. She looked great...damn it.

We both looked down the hall and Lydia was the first to notice a cleaning woman, the same person who turns down the sheets at bedtime. Lydia asked her for a sleep mask so that she could get ample rest. Insurance for a good night's sleep seemed like a good idea so I made the same request. We each gave the cleaning woman our room numbers and then headed toward the bar.

James met the two of us near the hotel lounge.

"You know," James began. "I heard that not only the passengers but also a lot of the staff on the boat is European. It's a little ironic that it takes people from across the Atlantic to get us to appreciate our Great Lakes."

I wondered out loud if the staff all spoke English.

"Oh honey," Lydia cooed. "Of course they all speak English. I heard the outlets in the cabins are European and you need those funny plug adjusters. That will probably be the only real adjusting we will have to do."

"I read about the European outlets in the brochure. That struck me as so odd."

James said the boats for this cruise are just like luxury ocean liners except they are built just for the Great Lakes especially to go through the Soo Locks.

Lydia asked, "What are the Soo Locks?"

James said, "In simple terms, a boat from higher Lake Superior goes into the Soo Locks and is able to safely go into the lower elevation of Lake Huron."

"How is that possible?" Lydia asked.

James said, "They place each boat in a holding tank, or "lock" and lower or raise the water, depending upon which lake the boat is headed to. I don't know a lot of the technical terms but thank God for the marvels of engineering. Because of that we'll be able to see all five of the Great Lakes."

James turned his attention back to the bar. He ordered all three of us warm mulled wine.

Lydia sat gracefully on the barstool. "I hear this is what they drink in Europe. How did you know?"

James just happened to like that drink. He wasn't being fashionable…he was just being James.

I thanked James for the drink. I wondered what the food on the boat would be like.

"Bea, where have you been hiding? Food on a cruise is one of the big attractions. It's always excellent and it's always available with at least a couple choices. I'm sure no matter what they prepare it will be fabulous." Lydia voice was louder than a whisper but still very quiet.

"Let's toast to our vacation." James raised his glass and said:

"May the seas be smooth. May the stars be bright. May our cruise be filled with comfort and delight."

Chapter Five

That night in my room I tried to give myself a crash course in mixing. How can I make small talk with James and sound casual as my heart is pounding inside my chest? What should I do? I start to think about Lydia. She's charming, attractive and bright. It's a waste of time to be jealous of her. We will be sharing this trip so it's best to think of ways to get along. Wouldn't a people person accept the colorful traveling ladies we saw at the hotel? So what if they are a little different? I sort of like eccentric people. They show personality. It's the cliques that drive me nuts.

Night One of the trip, spending the night in Toronto, got off to a good start. Just because I worry shouldn't detract from the reality that I was having fun already.

I didn't get a good night's sleep the first night. I was too excited about heading to the ship.

In the morning, as I was preparing to leave, I realized that I had more luggage than you can imagine. If I were flying they would have kicked me off the plane. Instead, the desk clerk saw my many bags and paged a bellboy. The bellboy practically had a hernia lifting all my belongings onto the cart. He was sweet though. He didn't complain.

The desk clerk then offered to call a cab for me. Since I had so much luggage, I didn't share a taxi with anyone.

The whole process took some time…well over 45 minutes from the time I set foot in the lobby until I was ready to leave. So by the time the cab got to the hotel, I was running late. I was going to meekly suggest to the cabbie that we try to get to the boat on time.

Instead, the hotel clerk told the cab driver to get me on board as fast as possible.

The cabbie took off and drove 70 miles per hour. My heart was in my throat the whole drive there. But, I will say this…the cab driver got me to the boat on time. In fact, I was one of the first to arrive.

Boarding the ship was Day Two on my itinerary. Little did I know such an innocent task, boarding the ship, could evoke such a wide range of emotions such as the sheer terror describing the cab ride and now standing awestruck in front of this vessel.

The boat was tied to a huge dock in Toronto. Some people had relatives there to see them off. I just waved and smiled. In fact, I couldn't wipe the smile off my face. Soon I'll be headed out to sea!

My heart raced. The boat was huge and beautiful. I would happily call this place home for the next week.

Just then James and Lydia emerged from another taxi. We said our hellos, and James and Lydia boarded the sea craft together. We were told the vessel was built as a luxury liner but made specifically for the Great Lakes.

I practically ran to my room and discovered that I've got a porthole for a view of the lakes. It had a TV and a private bath.

The storage here was ample. There were two single beds. It was quite nice. I love it although I don't plan on spending too much time in the cabin. I have a Lithuanian roommate who is never there. I met her briefly. She is tall with blonde hair and her English is excellent. It might even be better than mine. Her accent is pleasant to the ear. I'm sure I'll see her again back in the room soon enough.

The whole ship is an elegant piece of craftsmanship. Wood paneling is everywhere. It is six decks high and stands about 50 feet tall. It has a pool. It has a formal dining room serving breakfast, lunch and dinner. It is impressive. The waiters wear tuxedos and serve exquisite dishes of freshwater fish cooked to perfection or any entrée you could name. This was top notch.

The vessel also had a wine bar as well as nightly entertainment in the lounge. I was happy when I heard the ship had a fitness room and a sauna. This is an elegant craft. I also heard another passenger mention taking walks around the deck before breakfast to stay in shape. Who could argue with the scenery?

The liner also had a poolside bar. Whoever designed this ship thought of everything!

The crew told us we'd celebrate Oktoberfest on board the boat. That could be a lot of fun.

Everyone says that cruises are known for their food and I am excited about that. Then again, I don't want to leave this ship the size of the Titanic. Talk about a good trip gone sour! I need a plan. I'll commit to the daily walks on the top deck in the morning to keep fit. Eat, drink and exercise, in that order is what I'll do. Also, I suspected that many meals would feature fish. Not being fond of fish I may just lose weight. Nah! Who am I kidding?

You know I try so hard to think and do the right thing. What am I trying to do, be perfect? I'm afraid perfection is not in the stars for me. I'd gladly settle for having better social skills.

Then the kid inside of me gets thinking…James and Bea, Bea and James, yeah, I like the sound of that. But, I am not alone in my admiration for James.

Let's not forget Lydia. Lydia's pretty. Lydia's sweet. Lydia's cultured. Here I meet a nice man who doesn't make me feel nervous and Lydia steps in the picture.

Instead I'll try to make Uncle Ned proud. I'll try to focus on the beauty around me and not on the silly worries inside of me.

James will probably want to know what I do for a living. Which answer should I give him? I'm no longer a telemarketer. It's not an easy job. I could pretend to be independently wealthy. No, he won't buy that. I'll tell him I'm "in between positions."

I headed to the main deck trying to think positively. *No one ever died of embarrassment. Just make an effort to mix,* I told myself.

I was on the deck, soaking up the view and I saw them. "Hi James. Hi Lydia." There, that wasn't so hard.

"Hello Bea. How is it going Lydia?"

"Great!" Lydia replied.

"Lydia," I began. "You sense things. Don't you feel as if there is something very special about the Great Lakes?"

"What exactly do you mean?" asked Lydia.

"I feel as if this much fresh water in one place is…well, it's mystical. Don't you feel it too?" I asked.

"Does that make the Hoover dam mystical too?" James asked. Then James wiped the smirk off his face and remarked, "If you seek a pleasant peninsula, look about you."

"That's exactly what my uncle wrote in my note when he gave me these tickets," I said. "So you feel it, right James?"

"Longfellow and Hemingway aren't wrong," James agreed. "I feel it."

"I feel it too. It's enough to make your spine tingle." Lydia took a huge breath as if to soak it all in.

"I wouldn't go that far," James said.

I looked at James and smiled. He is unpretentious and funny. I really hope Lydia is too refined to take a serious interest in James.

I was glancing on the deck and saw an older couple holding hands. It was sweet to see someone still in love after all those years. I wish I could find someone to love and to grow old with.

The man pointed out to the water and his wife smiled. He put his arm around her as they leaned on the deck railing.

The wind was blowing so they didn't stay there long. But even as they walked away, they remained hand in hand.

Lydia said she wanted to get organized so she excused herself. That left James alone with me.

James is always joking around so I didn't get nervous around him. He didn't ask about my job. He surprised me by asking my favorite TV show.

"What year?"

"Of all time!"

"Now that's a hard one. So, what's YOUR favorite TV show?"

"I asked first." James ignored my question. He always makes me feel comfortable.

"Well, since we're on a cruise I'll pick Love Boat. I used to love that show." My thoughts suddenly turned to the ship named the Princess.

"Okay, obvious choice being on a cruise and all but I'll accept it until you start thinking more creatively." James walked as he talked.

"Your turn." I was trying to keep up with him as he strolled.

"I like the light stuff too. Let's see…Love Boat was an 80's show. How about Moonlighting? I liked that. Did you?"

"I thought that was great. Did you see the episode of the Taming of the Shrew? Those writers must have had fun." I laughed as I remembered Bruce Willis sticking his head through the door shouting, "Here's Petruchio!"

"Okay, so we've covered the not-so-distant past. What shows do you like now?" James asked and the topic was light. No need to sweat this one.

"I thought 'Titus' was hysterical but they took it off the air."

"Is? What IS your favorite show?"

"Gilmore Girls, without question. It's smart and funny. It's fast-paced but they play nice. There's nothing mean-spirited about it. Hard work pays off in that show. So do clever comebacks."

"I'll make a point to look for it." James slowed down his pace.

"It's worth it." I slowed down too.

"But not until AFTER the cruise."

"Thank God. What a waste to watch TV on a cruise!" As I said it I thought how many times I had turned to the television instead of getting out there and meeting people. Not this time!

"If you remember Moonlighting then how old are you?" James was being very direct for the first time.

"It's not proper to ask a lady her age."

"Oh, I see Lydia is having her influence on you. I'm sorry. It is a rude question. I was just trying to find some common ground. How about this…how far back do you remember TV?" James posed.

"I remember the moon landing." I didn't want to tell him I remembered Mighty Mouse cartoons.

"That's a no-brainer. Do you remember the Patty Duke show?" James asked.

"I remember part of the theme song." I was just about to start singing it when James spoke.

"Yes, but do you remember Patty's boyfriend's name?"

"No but I bet you do."

"Moose."

"As in chocolate or something you put in your hair?"

"No as in a big hunky football player." James smiled.

I like the fact that we're talking about television. There's no pretense in it. "Did we also witness these things from the same place? I grew up in Michigan. How about you James?"

"I was born at Virginia Beach but moved here as a little boy."

"So you said this could be a working vacation but you plan to have fun."

"Yep. I want to keep my eyes open to possibilities. I was thinking I might be able to do a calendar...you know, the fall colors, sunsets on the blue water, sandy beaches, giant white pines..."

"I'd buy one. Michigan is divided in two not only by the upper and lower peninsula but also in terms of the industrial side versus the great outdoors."

"I think most states share that trait of being home to both industry and nature. I just happen to think that Michigan's two sides —industry and nature—are more obvious than in most states." James started back up strolling around the deck again.

"Well get ready for lots of nature." I followed.

"Thanks to the marvels of industry—this elaborate sea craft, we can enjoy nature—the wonder that is the Great Lakes." James put out his hand as if to display the lakes.

"On beautiful days like today I am so inspired. When it's a nice day in Michigan it's one fabulous day. Just a trace of clouds in that blue, blue sky, isn't it exciting?" I looked up.

"I think this whole trip is exciting. Wait just a minute will you?" James stopped in his tracks.

"Sure. What's up?"

"I have to get something. I'll be right back." James headed toward his cabin.

"I'll just take in the scenery," I said.

I looked over the edge of the ship. The water was azure. It was the oddest sensation of feeling as if I was on the ocean but I knew no shore was too distant, even if it was out of sight. I knew no poisonous jellyfish would sting me. No sharks would attack me. If, God forbid, we had to use the lifeboats, I knew I would not die of dehydration. There was plenty of fresh water everywhere.

It's a good thing I didn't have to ponder these increasingly dramatic scenarios for too long before James returned. He had a small duffel bag that looked pretty heavy.

He got out one of his cameras and a huge lens. He started snapping photos and then looking at the back end of the camera.

I asked what he was doing. He said he had a digital camera and he was able to see how the photos would turn out.

He showed me. I'm not sure how he did it but James managed to capture the blueness of the sky, the vastness of the water and the sense of tranquility it brought. At least that's what the little square looked like. It was hard to tell.

He told me to stand beside the rail. I did. He said he'd take the picture on the count of three. I closed my eyes. He tried it again…one, two, three…"Nope that's not the look yet," he said.

I was just about to tell him "Wait a minute, buddy," when he started snapping photos. I yelled for him to stop but he laughed and kept taking my picture.

I mockingly shook my fist at him. Snap, snap, snap, he got it all on film.

Oh how I wished I had my camera with me. I'd show him.

The fact that he kept taking photos even when I was at my worst made me laugh. He stopped.

"Hey, why not capture THAT smile? It was real enough," I asked.

"Because." And he kissed me.

I forgot all about the photos. I was startled but certainly not upset.

The kiss seemed natural enough. I didn't have time to ponder the issue because Lydia came within view. She didn't see the kiss. She walked up to James with a huge smile.

"Is your camera ready for ME?" Lydia asked.

"It can handle whatever you dish out," James replied.

Just then a breeze made Lydia's hair completely cover her face. James captured it on film.

"Oh no you don't," Lydia warned with a no-kidding voice.

"Consider it erased. Look. See?" James showed Lydia the photos on the back and the one of her was gone.

"What is your favorite subject matter?" Lydia asked.

"I love the outdoors. I like the fall colors." James reached down into his duffel bag.

"Well, that has mass appeal but critics don't like clichés."

"Some things are popular for a good reason." James found what he was looking for.

"You've got me there." Lydia succumbed to the magic of the sights.

Chapter Six

"I heard that we might have a scavenger hunt. We get clues and have to search for the answers. Did either of you hear anything about that?" I wanted to participate.

"I did." The tone of James's voice didn't reveal if he was excited about the scavenger hunt or not.

"How many are on a team?" Lydia queried.

"Just look out there, will you. There it is...beautiful blue water wherever you look." James was more absorbed in the scenery than in the conversation. "It kind of makes all the extra activities seem superfluous."

"Well, if they allow three on a team, I think we've got a group right here." I was looking at the autumn shoreline as I spoke.

"Sounds good to me." Lydia nodded.

"It could be a good way to learn." James seemed to give us his full attention again.

"Who said anything about learning? I'm here to have fun!" I smiled broadly to emphasize my point. Besides, I couldn't stop smiling if I tried. I was slowly starting to relax and enjoy myself.

Since this boat was smaller than an ocean liner we had a cruise director but she wasn't intent on keeping everyone busy every minute.

The scavenger hunt was optional. Some people thought it was a dumb idea.

"Glad they aren't playing then." James was a good sport and didn't feel like joining forces with complainers.

"I agree," Lydia intoned. "If people didn't want to take part but they were forced to join, they'd just ruin it with a bad attitude. This hunt could be fun. This isn't the time to be sophisticated."

"Well," James said. "No need to worry about sophisticates here. I'm a big kid at heart. It sounds like fun to me."

My heart melted. James is a good sport. He doesn't worry more about appearances than having fun. I felt like shouting "I'm a big kid too, James! Look! Look here! I'm a big kid too." But I didn't.

"Maybe we'll hear more about it later on today." Lydia suggested. "I guess it's about time to get dressed for dinner. Isn't tonight the big event?" If I looked puzzled it was because I felt puzzled. This was our first night at sea and in a way it felt as if we'd been together for quite a while.

"Yes. Tonight we attend the Captain's Welcome Party. I'm sure we'll get a better feel for the voyage after the soiree." Lydia straightened her posture.

"What are you wearing tonight?" I had to ask Lydia. She would know how to dress. "And what time does it start?"

"It starts at seven in the restaurant and I'm wearing a coat and tie," James said.

Lydia straightened out the invisible wrinkles in her outfit as she spoke. "If only it were that easy for women."

"Oh relax." James looked impatient but tolerant. "This whole cruise is casual."

"Even the natural look takes effort." Lydia spoke the truth.

It wasn't just the two of us who agreed upon this. I remember discovering the fine art of the natural look in college. It took one full hour to look as if you wore no make-up whatsoever.

"Well, if I'm going to look at all presentable I'd better head to my cabin and start getting ready for tonight's big event," I excused myself.

As I walked in my door, my Lithuanian roommate was there. Thank God her English is good because my Lithuanian is a little lacking.

Her name is Yura. Yura is sweet. She asked if I'm having a nice time so far. I said an emphatic yes. She said she was enjoying herself too. She had met a nice German gentleman and enjoyed his company. I guess with both of them being from Europe it gave them a sense of familiarity. Yura was just leaving as I entered. She mentioned that she'd look for me upstairs.

We had barely set sail and I was excited. I carefully smoothed out my dress and suddenly felt quite stylish. It was a black dress that wrapped around the waist and tied on the side. While I was content with my outfit I was feeling a little uncomfortable. I was nervous about meeting all sorts of new people. But, I'm here to have fun.

This trip is a real thrill for me. I'd be foolish to retreat when I feel excitement. And I can say quite honestly that my enthusiasm is genuine.

I just put the finishing touches on my hair, patted my make-up with lightly wet fingers to let it set (an old trick I'd learned from years of reading Glamour magazine) and I headed up to the dining room.

The schedule was a cocktail party followed by dinner. I wasn't nervous about dinner. I was hungry. As I entered the dining salon, I saw Lydia talking to a good-looking gentleman. He seemed pleasant. He seemed quite taken with Lydia. Her charm was smooth. Her sweetness was sincere. Perhaps the two of them would hit it off.

Just then James came up to me and handed me a glass of punch. He looked attractive in his sports jacket.

I kidded James that he should take pictures at the party and sell them. I said he should become the ship's photographer.

James laughed and said he could wait until everyone had too much to drink and then take photos. Then he could become the ship's black-mailer.

After a bit of socializing and drinking the Captain stood up and spoke to the group. To break the ice he said, "Call me Captain Bill. I don't go in for formality much but I do like a top notch cruise."

He welcomed us aboard and said we were in for a treat. Captain Bill told us that he had sailed the ocean and now he had been on the Great Lakes for the past eight years. He added that he regretted to say that this would be his last time steering the liner through the Great Lakes because he is headed back to ocean liners after this trip.

But, the captain noted, that was in the future and as for now, our mission was to enjoy this trip as much as possible. He assured us we would be delighted.

The captain mentioned that for those interested, we would be having a scavenger hunt. He assured us that he would not treat us like children at camp but it would be a fun way to learn about the area and to unravel clues about the sights around us. He asked how many people had ever been on a road rally. A few smiled. He said this scavenger hunt was like that...simple and fun.

He said those not interested were encouraged not to participate. He welcomed people to attend lectures about the Great Lakes. Captain Bill emphasized that this trip was about having a good time. He told us to forget televisions and computers and phones. Instead, he said, get to know the people on board. He added that it looked as if we were off to a good start.

Captain Bill didn't speak that long and a band started playing dinner music.

The group sort of moved around cautiously at first. Caution was soon dropped after a few glasses of wine from one of the many Great Lakes wineries and after a few appetizers such as water chestnuts wrapped with bacon. People started to mix a little. The original silence was filled with a constant hum. People seemed to be enjoying themselves.

James and I sipped wine and thought we'd leave Lydia alone with her handsome new friend for a minute or two.

We noticed the ladies we saw in the hotel in Toronto and they looked positively elegant. Any trace of anger between them was long gone.

Usually a cruise attracts more women than men. This cruise had a lot of couples. Single people seem to pair off when they first meet and are otherwise unaccompanied. It is an instinctive measure to feel safe and relaxed. Being alone with a group of strangers can cause a heightened state of nerves. Once you buddy up with someone, no matter how tentatively, you don't have that terrible feeling of total solitude.

I'm not sure if my attraction to James was to stave off fear of feeling alone or if I saw something special in him. I think it was a little of both. He's nice. He's here. And he's pleasant.

As for the rest of the ship pairing off, as I said, it was instinctive. When I say the group coupled up, what I really mean is they each found a pal, someone stable in this constant stream of new experiences. It wasn't so much a boy-girl thing as it was finding a friendly face to whom you could return consistently throughout the trip as an anchor. These weren't lasting friendships. They were symbiotic friends for the length of the trip.

At first I was afraid that Lydia would be a permanent fixture on my vacation. For the time being though it seemed as if Lydia had met someone who appreciated her charm.

James and I joined Lydia and her new friend, Albert, for dinner. Our first dinner on board was a buffet. It had every item you can think of and a few more to spare. The perch got the highest compliments. I opted for something without gills, namely Chicken Fra Angelica. It was superb.

Lydia wore a rusty suede skirt and a matching silk blouse. She couldn't have chosen a better outfit to explore the Great Lakes in style. Now that she is in the good company with another, I can admit that I was jealous of her. She is so together. I am a bit shy. She is worldly. I am not. She is kind to me and even that bothered me. At first I foolishly took her kindness to me to be patronizing. Yet I wasn't confident in a new situation so I was almost glad for that extra help and dose of patience. After mulling all of this over, the simple truth hit me...Lydia is genuinely nice. When things go well it's easy to see how I made silly assumptions. This was a time when I didn't mind being wrong.

James' nonstop ribbing takes the edge off so I don't worry so much about being anyone but myself. We had already talked and found some things in common. I know that liking the same television shows is hardly the basis for much of a relationship but I am on board this vessel for six nights. Having a relationship is not a part of the program anyway. But it did my heart good to think I'd be spending this trip of a lifetime with someone as amiable as James.

Some of the couples started dancing to the band. These were real couples. They were in love long before they even heard of this cruise. It was touching to see some older couples, folks who had been with one another for so many years, dancing and anticipating the other's moves, swaying in a way that only years of practice together can provide.

I looked up and Lydia was on the dance floor too. She looked elegant and refined. Albert was a good dancer. Lydia and he looked graceful on the floor as they effortlessly spun and turned, keeping up with the beat in smooth steps.

Do I dare look longingly at James as if to beg him to dance with me? James was chatting with some other women as I had my eyes on the dance floor. Just because we had buddied-up didn't mean that he was interested in me exclusively.

When will men understand that women are forever grateful if shown a little consideration? When will they figure out that if men think of what might please us, and dive into it with enthusiasm that the payback is honest and generous gratitude? When will James ask me to dance?

I headed to the bar and ordered bottled water as James came up from behind me. I barely had the beverage in my hand when he set my drink down and pulled on my hand as he led me to the dance floor. Without being asked, without a nudge at all, this sweet and handsome man had somehow read my mind and had me twirling around both physically and emotionally. I was delighted.

He didn't step on my toes once and I wish I could say that I returned the favor. Thank God for thick shoes and kind hearts. This evening was progressing along nicely.

I don't know how long we were on the dance floor before Lydia's friend, Albert, came up to me and asked me to dance. I had a feeling Lydia was behind that gesture. James asked Lydia to dance. I had the feeling that Lydia was behind that gesture as well.

Albert was older than James, and he was refined, much like Lydia. Conversation came easily to him and not much seemed to bother him, including my clumsy feet. He spoke of the trip and mentioned that he had been on this cruise before, stating that he loved it. Albert said this was certainly the best time of year for this cruise because of the fall colors and moderate temperatures.

Albert and I got talking some more and it turns out that he played bridge to pay his way through college. He is a life master in bridge. He asked if either James or I played bridge and I said a firm no. I knew enough about bridge to know that Albert was part of a very small group of accomplished players. I was not about to bid my first hand with someone who attained the highest ranking in bridge.

I asked Albert if Lydia played bridge and he said yes and his face lit up as he stated that. "It was one of the first questions I asked her. She says she's a little rusty but I am looking for another couple for a foursome."

"Well count me out. But I'm sure you'll find others who will join you." I'm not much of a card player.

The night was growing old and it was near the end of the band's set when the singer grabbed the microphone and said they were about to play the last song of the evening. She kindly stated that those who had yet to grace the dance floor might want to consider doing so now.

I was delighted to see the older women we had seen a few times since the hotel in Toronto were asked to dance.

These older women seemed transformed into lovely ladies waltzing as if they were royalty. One might have been Cinderella, dancing with her prince. With the other, I felt like I was watching Anna and the King of Siam.

James found me for the last dance. He held me closely to him this time, not saying a word. If James thought this wasn't a time for words I didn't want to tell him otherwise. The silence enhanced the closeness of the dancing.

I glanced over at Lydia and Albert. He was whispering to her and she was giggling. *Good,* I thought. They make a nice pair. They have a lot in common.

After the band stopped and the room silently emptied I said goodnight to James as he walked me down to my cabin. As I entered the cabin I realized Yura, my Lithuanian roommate, was already sound asleep.

I pulled out a picture of Uncle Ned. One thing my mother had given me for the trip was a journal so that I could share my stories with Ned when I got home.

What should I say in my first journal entry, this second day of my trip?

"Trip is going to be great. Nice people. I'm amazed that strangers can become fast friends when forced to do so."

No. That didn't seem like the type of entry Uncle Ned would appreciate.

I wrote, "Who could believe that something so close to my home has such majesty? I've only spent a short time on the boat and have seen the bluest of waters, the clearest of skies and met the kindest of people. The trip has just started and already I'm afraid it will end too soon. But I feel lucky for this chance to see what I've taken for granted for so long."

I tucked the journal into my canvas tote and went to bed. It had been one of the longest days I could remember because so much had happened. And yet the day had flown by because so much had happened.

Chapter Seven

"Get up," Yura said. "It's time to exercise."

"No. It's the middle of the night," I moaned.

Yura's voice got louder. "Oh no it's not, it's seven a.m. and it's time for you to get up and walk."

"Where am I?" I was confused.

"Don't be silly. You're in the middle of Lake Ontario. Come on now. Don't be lazy. Get up."

I glanced at the clock; it read seven a.m. I groaned, put the pillow over my head for half a minute and then got up. This is how I started my second day at sea.

Being on the deck meant feeling the chilly wind off the water. At first I just dragged myself around the deck. I was a sorry sight to see. Then the nip in the air helped me break into a brisk walk. I wasn't counting the number of laps I did but I did break a sweat. I figured that was good enough for today.

I was surprised to see just how many people had decided to get a little exercise. I looked around and saw the older ladies. I nicknamed them Velma and Louise figuring it sounded like a tamer and older version of Thelma and Louise. They were in sweat suits just like everybody else. They kept up with the pace.

As I walked around the deck I couldn't help but marvel at the water and the horizon. I could hear the water gently lapping against the side of the ship. I've always thought that water had almost a musical sound. Currently we are on Lake Ontario. Lake Ontario is the one Great Lake not bordering Michigan. It covers an area of 7,300 square miles. It has an average depth of 606 feet and it's 190 miles long. We are traversing Lake Ontario and soon we'll see Niagara Falls.

A few trees had started to change color. With the wind and water and weather I couldn't help but think that this is what perfection looks like. I tried to memorize the view and the feeling. I wonder what good old Uncle Ned thought the first time he saw these sights. Did he have time to gather in the beauty while working on a freighter?

After my brisk walk around the deck I went straight to the dining room for breakfast. Nobody cared that I was wearing my sweats. In fact it was almost a status symbol because those of us dripping in sweats had proven that we had the willpower to stay fit.

Staying fit doesn't mean giving up good food. I could diet the rest of my life but this cruise only lasted one week. I wouldn't eat until I hurt but it wouldn't hurt to enjoy myself.

I found myself at the buffet table with a plate that started with fresh fruit and kept amassing more and more food. A crepe here…an omelet there…and of course I had to try their Belgian waffles.

Some people were already seated. I didn't see Lydia among the group. James was not to be seen either.

I wasn't worried about not seeing James. I figured he was sleeping in during a much-deserved vacation.

I joined the elderly women at their table and introduced myself. They remembered me from the hotel. It turns out their names were not Velma and Louise but rather Edith and Helen.

They seemed pleasant. They knew each other before the trip and decided to enjoy their vacations together. Each had been married long ago, each had buried her husband long ago, and long ago each had children who are now well into their adult years.

"We decided to enjoy our golden years," Edith said. "We are neighbors at home and when Helen got the brochure she ran right over to show it to me. We reserved our suite as soon as we could. We've been waiting for this trip for over a year now."

Helen said, "It's even better than I pictured. I've traveled quite a bit but this is something of a rare treat. It's not very often you get to see how beautiful your own state is while in the lap of luxury."

They asked if I was married. I said no. They asked if I had ever been married. I said no. They asked if I wanted to get married. I said that first I need to find the right man.

Helen put her hand to her mouth as Edith raised an eyebrow.

"Any suggestions?" I asked.

"Oh no, dear. Just enjoy this trip. We know we plan to savor it," they chimed.

After we all enjoyed a feast, I pushed myself away from the table to stop me from devouring any more food. As I did, Helen and Edith started talking quietly and quickly.

They seemed friendly enough. I could easily picture both of them gossiping, at least with each other, but I couldn't ever picture any malice in their remarks. So regardless of what they were saying as I walked away from the table I knew it was inoffensive.

I went back to my room, showered, changed and got ready for the rest of the day.

I went back up on deck as they were still serving breakfast. I saw James; he asked me to join him, which I did. He seemed cheerful first thing in the morning and I liked that.

"Top of the morning to you," James smiled.

"And to you," I smiled back.

James started, "I haven't slept this well in years. I think I've come down with a case of hobo malaria."

I stood back a little bit looking worried.

James went on and explained, "Hobo malaria just means that I don't feel like doing anything."

The sea air causes hobo malaria, according to James, and it makes you sleep like a baby. It drains you of all ambition. Once stricken it takes all your effort to get out of bed.

I liked the expression of "hobo malaria" because it was something that my Uncle Ned would have said. For a second I wondered what Uncle Ned would think of James. While they were different from one another, I adored them both.

Some people can't adjust to a new environment. James seemed to be comfortable no matter where he went or with whom he was speaking. He was happy in his own skin and happy around just about everybody.

Soon after breakfast a crewmember announced that those interested in the scavenger hunt were to appear on deck. It was not a required event but just a whimsical way to enjoy the sights. James and I stood together. We had already agreed we would be a team. Lydia and Albert decided to be a team too. Teams could be two or three people. Lydia and Albert decided it would be more fun to compete against us then to work with us. We agreed. We were up to their challenge.

As we sailed across Lake Ontario, our first stop was to be Niagara Falls and the Welland Canal. Our first clue for the scavenger hunt said:

> *Toronto is a world-class city.*
> *Get a postcard of the Horseshoe Falls pretty.*
> *Make sure a rainbow is in the mist.*
> *That's the first item on your list.*

The ship pulled into port briefly and many folks dashed for the nearest souvenir shop.

James looked around and noticed another store near The Falls that wasn't brimming with people. We approached the vendor who had the perfect postcard.

"That will be one dollar, American." The shop owner held out his hand for payment.

James handed him the bill and said "Thank you." He then approached me saying, "This isn't too bad so far. Before we go, stand in front of the falls and I'll get a picture of you."

I tried my best fake smile but James saw right through it and would have none of it. Frustrated, I wrinkled my nose and that's when he took the shot.

I said, "I suppose this falls under the category of realistic. Why don't you just knock on my door at five AM and catch me before I'm fully awake?"

I was teasing and thank goodness James realized it. "Don't tempt me," he warned.

We weren't there very long before we got the signal that it was time to board the ship again.

A small line formed to enter the boat and then we were back on the lake in no time.

We saw Lydia and Albert smiling. Albert held a postcard above his head. They made it clear from the start that we were the team they wanted to beat.

Chapter Eight

Day Three at sea and the entire day will be spent on Lake Erie. Lake Erie is 250 miles long. It is only an average of 120 feet deep and its area is about 10,000 square miles. Passing through the Welland Canal was unlike anything I've done before. Yet being on Lake Erie felt like being on an ocean.

We saw lots of fishing boats and pleasure crafts. It was a beautiful day. The air from the water was crisp and cool but the sun made the breeze welcome.

James and I sat on deck and I told him some of my stories about Uncle Ned on the freighters. He listened with interest. He said he'd like to meet my uncle sometime.

James said, "I've got an Aunt Eudora who is so full of life she dived in a swimming pool with her clothes on. She doesn't want to miss any opportunity life has to offer. At the time she was in her seventies. The day was hot. The pool was cool. She took off her jewelry and jumped right in."

"If I did that I'd probably drown," I said.

James just laughed and said, "I think there is only room for one Aunt Eudora in this world. She's done other things like send us chocolate covered grasshoppers as gifts. She's one of a kind. And maybe that's a good thing."

"What would she do if she were on this cruise?" I asked.

"You mean AFTER she went over Niagara Falls in a barrel?" James said. "Your Uncle Ned sounds a little bit tamer," James continued.

"Yes and no," I said. "His mother made cherry bounce in the bathtub."

"What in the world is cherry bounce?"

"It's the sweetened equivalent of bathtub gin. No one in the family wanted to give up liquor during Prohibition. So they got it the old-fashioned way…they made it."

"Aunt Eudora would drink cherry bounce."

"Uncle Ned tells stories that he heard as a boy about how people drove across the frozen Detroit River during the winter. They drove from Canada, loading their cars with liquor. Detroit wasn't exactly a dry town during the Twenties." I acted like I really knew. I was just reciting what I had heard.

"What town was?" James asked.

"What time is it? It must be happy hour somewhere?" I asked.

"I'll give you happy hour!" James smiled and pulled me close to him. He kissed me gently.

"I suppose you think that is intoxicating!" I said.

"No I call it 'chemistry,'" James said. I became silent. I didn't know what was going to happen next.

James laced his arm in mine and we strolled around the deck. I had such a warm feeling from it. It was so innocent and so connected at the same time.

* * * * *

We had leisurely traveled across Lake Erie and now we were going through the Detroit River to Lake St. Clair. From there we took the St. Clair River to Port Huron.

We glided under the Blue Water Bridge connecting Michigan to Canada. All sorts of boats were on the water: every type of pleasure craft, speedboats, yachts, sail boats and freighters.

A crewmember announced that more domestic and international freighters pass under this bridge than through both the Suez and Panama Canal combined.

While James and I found that interesting, we had a mission. Our next clue had to do with the port of call in Port Huron.

The clue read:

A genius bright and true
Lived his boyhood near waters blue.
Stop by his namesake Inn
For a book of matches
To help you win.

James said, "Let me see that brochure. Okay, 'Port Huron…home to lovely shops and sights…sailboats…nice riverfront…'"

"I guess we get off and look around. We could go to the phone book and look up inns and hotels to see if any bear the name of a genius," I suggested.

"Not such a bad plan," James agreed.

The ship pulled into port. Some folks got off and headed toward restaurants with waterfront views. Others were like us, in search of the answer on the scavenger hunt.

We decided to do both. James and I walked to a café with a view of the water. It was smaller than most of the restaurants in the immediate area but it had a cozy feel about it.

James ordered a coffee and I felt like having a cup of peppermint tea. The waiter was pleasant and quickly brought both drinks.

As the waiter was walking away James asked him if anyone famous ever lived in Port Huron.

The waiter said, "Thomas Edison. You can't help but see his name all over town."

"Aha! All we have to do is find the Thomas Edison Inn!" James exclaimed.

The waiter heard that remark and said it was within walking distance of the café. All we had to do was walk a few blocks down the waterfront promenade and we would see an English Tudor inn facing the St. Clair River.

James didn't rush me. I wanted to enjoy every sip of my tea and I liked looking at the river.

But eventually we got up and walked the scenic path to the Inn.

The Thomas Edison Inn is beautiful. It's tasteful without being stuffy. We walked in, looking very much like tourists, and approached the front desk.

I was looking for matchbooks everywhere I could in the lobby. I couldn't find a one.

Then I heard Lydia giggle from the bar. We went in and saw Lydia and Albert enjoying a glass of something. They didn't see us approach them.

I saw a large glass bowl full of matches and took a handful. I don't know what possessed me to take so many but my only regret at the time was that I didn't have bigger hands. I really wanted those matches.

James was the polite one and said hello to Lydia and Albert.

"Have any trouble finding the place?" Albert asked James.

"No, but clearly you got here before we did. How did you know where to go?"

"I kept a copy of the cruise brochure. I flipped the sheet over and saw that some travelers boarded in Port Huron and spent the prior night at the Thomas Edison Inn. It's on there. Once I got the name it was just a matter of asking for directions. Did you get your book of matches yet?"

"I'm just about to do that." James looked for some matches on the bar.

I didn't want to reveal that I already had acquired a bulky clump of matchbooks. James found a book and tucked it in his pocket.

Regarding Albert and Lydia's prowess for finding the inn, James was not about to admit it but we had that same brochure as Lydia and Albert. He never bothered to look at the entire thing.

The competition between our two teams was completely friendly. I don't think James was used to losing and Albert was accustomed to winning. I looked up and saw them in the middle of a very short stare down. It was cute.

Neither really cared so much about the scavenger hunt or the results except that it was a challenge and a diversion.

But both James and Albert talked it up like it was a big deal. James kept telling Albert not to clear shelf space for the prize just yet.

Albert countered with saying, "May the best man win" and then putting his hand to his head and saying, "Oh, that's me!"

Lydia and I smiled.

Chapter Nine

Translate this Latin saying
For the third clue
In this game that you're playing...
"Si quaeris peninsulam amoenan circumspice. "

"Who speaks Latin?" James asked. James didn't. I sure didn't.
I saw Lydia and Albert lean together for a quick huddle. I could hear, "I think 'si' means 'if' or 'yes,' I'm not sure which one it is."
"Let's find the ship's doctor!" I shouted. I wished I hadn't said it so loudly because people followed us.
James and I ran toward the ship's infirmary. We found the doctor and quickly placed the phrase in front of him.
He started mumbling. "I'm sorry," he said. "These are not medical terms. It's been a long time since I had Latin."
I tugged on James shirt and he leaned down. I whispered to him that we try the library.
Other folks were still trying to piece the saying together with the ship's doctor. He was slowly making progress but we knew that he would only be of so much help. After all, it was a hunt and it was up to the passengers to discover the answers.
James and I headed for the library. No one was in there. The room was a nice size and held many volumes. We searched for a Latin dictionary. James kept looking for that while I tried an ancient unabridged dictionary and went to the foreign phrases section.
No luck there. Then I saw an old book of Michigan's history. I

don't know why I opened it up except that the cover looked inviting. I found on the first page: *"Si quaeris peninsulam amoenan circumspice."* It means, "If you seek a pleasant peninsula, look about you—Michigan's sate motto."

"We've got it!" I shouted.

James was pleased. He also wondered how everyone else was faring on the topic. Did the doctor crack the code? Did the ship's doctor send people to all sorts of crew members to piece the saying together? We saw some people scurry and search while others took it slowly, the way some spend a leisurely Sunday doing a crossword puzzle. Many folks on board had studied Latin. It was just a matter of time before they solved the riddle.

We brought our translation to Amanda, the cruise director in charge of the scavenger hunt. While it was the ship's captain who originally spoke of the scavenger hunt, Amanda was in charge of organizing the activity and verifying the answers. When we brought our solution to Amanda she said that we were the first to figure it out.

"Now that you've done that," Amanda suggested. "Why not enjoy the rest of the day?"

"Can't you give us the next clue?" I was jazzed.

"Pace yourself," Amanda smiled amiably.

"That was kind of exciting." I squeezed James' hand.

James smiled at me and then laughed. "Sure it was fun. Now let's look out at the real reason we're here. Isn't it beautiful?"

"What?"

"Do you have to ask?" James looked at me with disbelief.

"Oh, you mean being on a cruise in the Great Lakes during the color season. It's cool."

We both knew "cool" didn't begin to describe the serene scenery. I had grossly understated the situation. The rich colors looked as if an artist had painted the trees and shoreline just for our benefit. The leaves were ablaze with color. At that moment I didn't want to be anywhere else on the planet. This was as close to perfection as it comes.

We both leaned on the ship's railing. We both pulled up deck chairs and a blanket. James put his arm around me as he draped the blanket around my shoulders. I wiggled in closer to him.

The view looked nicer than a postcard. We have lots of cloudy days in Michigan but on days when the sun shines—look out. The sky is a clear soft blue. The water seems like a jewel of lapis lazuli because of deep, rich blues. And the colors on the trees seem to glow. It is as if they absorb and reflect more light in the autumn than when the leaves are green.

Autumn has a smell. If you are in the woods in autumn, you smell the musky perfume of nature.

The breeze from the lakes, especially away from cities and towns, is so pure that it's almost intoxicating. It's not a smell so much as an elixir. You are immediately invigorated.

James reached in his bag and pulled something out. Within seconds his nose was in a book. Suddenly he spoke aloud and volunteered this piece of information. "We all know the Great Lakes were formed by glaciers. What most people don't know is that 'the last of the Michigan glaciers retreated about 12,000 years ago leaving glacial puddles, some as deep as 1,000 feet. These puddles filled in with water and became lakes.'"

"But there's more to it than that. I see here that 'about 200 million years ago salt-water seas covered the Great Lakes areas. When the seas disappeared they left a very soft seabed made of sand and fossilized sea life. The fossilized sea life is now known as the Petoskey Stone, which is Michigan's State Stone.'"

"'As the glaciers retreated and crossed paths with this soft seabed of sand and fossils, the glacier was able to dig much deeper than if it were retreating from non-porous rock. It was called a soft Paleozoic seabed and that's the reason why the glaciers dug the Great Lakes in their particular location.'"

"What does 'Paleozoic' mean?" I had never heard that word before.

"Let's look it up…" James said. "…It means the geologic time from about 590 million years ago to approximately 240 million years ago. I'm not a geologist so I don't know if I gave you enough information. I see here that the Paleozoic era came in between the Precambrian and the Mesozoic era. Did I tell you enough?"

"More than enough. I never knew that. I'm not sure I understand it." I sighed because I got to see what James was talking about, the wonders that are the Great Lakes, right in front of me. It sure beat sitting in a classroom listening to a professor drone on. Being on the lakes, soaking up the sunshine, breathing in the air, hearing all the seagulls, and seeing the magnificent shoreline was an experience no lecture could offer.

We sat and absorbed the sights for a while. The silence wasn't uncomfortable but I broke it anyway.

"So Professor, what are you thinking now?" I asked.

"Why do people ask that question? Is it possible to think about nothing? I don't know what I'm thinking. Maybe that a beer would make this just about perfect."

"So you are content otherwise?" I questioned.

"Content isn't a strong enough word. I'm in bliss," James said.

"Bliss?" My mind wandered as I said the word in my head. James is happy. And I am here. James is happy when I am with him. *I'm in bliss too!* I thought.

But what I said was, "Would you rather have a beer or kiss me right now?"

"Does it have to be one or the other? Can't it be both?"

"Of course it can. Sit tight." I got up and headed to the bar for a few beers. I wanted James to be as happy as possible. And here's why...I couldn't have dreamed up a nicer man. He's better than any checklist of good traits. He's a living, breathing, interacting wonderful human. I have always heard a woman shouldn't try to change a man. Not that I had given it a lot of thought but I can't think of one thing that I would change about James. He's not perfect and I like that.

Sometimes his jokes are corny and I love that he tries to be funny. He gets out there and tries. And sometimes he really makes me laugh, aloud!

"Two bottles of beer," I said.

"Any specific kind?" The bartender asked.

"Why don't you surprise me with what you think is good? Just make sure they are cold and in a bottle."

The bartender handed me two beers. I didn't recognize the label but that doesn't mean much.

I went back to James who was all curled up in the blanket. He saw me coming and he grinned broadly. Was he happy to see me or was it the beer? Oh forget it. As he said, does it have to be one or the other?

"Just because you got me a beer doesn't mean I forgot about that kiss." James pulled me to him. "In fact, it makes me want to kiss you that much more. You're sweet."

He hugged me. I like hugs. It was a big warm tight hug. We sipped our beers for a while and he planted a wet one right on my lips. He caught me by surprise.

But a beer kiss is not soft like a romantic kiss. I don't mean to pick it apart. We're having a great time and we don't have to make-out like teenagers.

We spent a few hours on the deck, arms wrapped around each other, blanket shared between us, listening to the sound of the water lapping up against the ship. The hum of the engine was faint. Louder than the engine were the cries of the squabbling seagulls circling the boat.

James mentioned, "I hope we don't have a constant flock of seagulls with us all the time."

"I don't mind them," I said. "I like them. They make it official that we are at sea."

"Bea at Sea..." James murmured.

"Yes that's me...Bea at Sea. Anne Morrow Lindberg celebrates the shoreline. I celebrate the Great Lakes."

"Oh, have you been writing poetry in your spare time?" James asked sarcastically.

"No, nothing so profound or flowery. I started to keep a journal so that I wouldn't forget anything. I want to tell my Uncle Ned all about this trip."

"He'll appreciate that. What a generous gift he gave you. I'd like to add that I'm especially glad your Uncle Ned is so giving."

"Why? He's kind but you're a total stranger. I don't see how his generosity would have an effect on you."

"Because of him I met you."

"Oh, sure, that's what you say now. Let's see how you feel after we've been at sea for a few days."

"I don't think I'll change my mind," James smiled.

I felt good as he said that.

We just came upon Lake Huron. Lake Huron averages a depth of 350 feet. It's about 280 miles long and covers an area of about 23,800 square miles. It's the second largest of the Great Lakes.

"Traveling on Lake Huron like this is so beautiful. When I was a little girl we had a cottage on the tip of the thumb of Michigan. The marker that divided Saginaw Bay and Lake Huron was in our back yard. We were little then and my dad took us to two islands about half an hour away by our motorboat. They were called the Charity Islands. There was Big Charity and Little Charity. One of the islands had an abandon lighthouse. One day we pulled the boat on shore and climbed the lighthouse. When we got to the top there was a sleeping bag there," I recounted.

"Did the sleeping bag belong to someone who wanted to live in the lighthouse or was it just some adventuresome traveler?"

"I don't know. We didn't really stay around to find out. Still, it was exciting. I remember riding on the boat fast and hitting the waves. If there were whitecaps the boat would kind of jump. It could be a choppy ride and the wind would really blow us all over the place. We had to sit tight in the boat." My words brought me back.

"That sounds like a vivid memory," James mused.

"Funny how the smallest detail of childhood becomes a treasure as an adult. I don't think I realized at the time I was in the boat that I was living what would become a fond memory." I spoke quietly almost as if I were speaking more to myself than to James. Of course James heard me and responded.

"The nicest memories are the ones that unfold during an event and pleasantly surprise you," James mentioned.

"Yeah, I guess you're right. I wonder how this trip will play out in each of our mind's eye once this voyage is finished?" I asked.

"I'm sure it will be filled with golden moments. This moment is nice," James sighed.

Chapter Ten

"Folks, if I may have your attention for a minute."

The announcement came in the main dining room. It got everyone's attention. No one knew what to expect.

"Soon we'll be spending Day Four at Little Current, Ontario. It is the island in the middle of Lake Huron between the mitt of Michigan and the shores of Ontario. That small passage is called the North Channel. We'll be able to see the North Channel but we won't travel through it. Just south of the North Channel is the Georgian Bay."

James quietly told me, "This land is loved by hunters and conservationists. It is almost as untouched as when the Native Americans lived here."

As we looked at the land I could see what James meant. The lakeside had rocks that jutted out of the shoreline. The water was as smooth as a mirror. We saw an old lighthouse that we were told was functional. It was whitewashed cement with a red cap.

A small house was attached that was hidden from view by the much larger lighthouse.

Amanda approached the group and it seemed as if she appeared out of nowhere. "We have another clue for those of you interested in the Scavenger Hunt. So far the teams are pretty close. So don't give up yet. We have a lot to go before this adventure is complete."

The Scavenger Hunters have the following clue:

At Little Current you will see
A lighthouse quaint as it can be
Name which state has the most

Lighthouses that dot its coast
As a bonus to this clever quest
Name the number it does possess.

I heard Albert mutter to Lydia, "How the hell are we supposed to come up with that?"

Lydia said, "Now, I know you have fun with this hunt. You're just upset because you lost at bridge last night."

"I didn't lose!" Albert quietly shouted. "He quit just before I was about to make a slam. Do you know how frustrating that is?"

"No," said Lydia. "But I do know I've never seen you this upset. You know, if this is as bad as it gets, you're not such a bad guy."

"He quit before I had a grand slam!" Albert muttered.

"Well, let's catch up on this leg of the scavenger hunt." Lydia tried to calm Albert down. "I know it's just good fun but I'd love to beat James and Bea. They make a cute couple, don't you think?"

"It was a grand slam!"

"Let it go."

"You're right. I agree. I think James and Bea look cute together. He told me when we first got on board that he was interested in her. Now, how in the world are we going to find out which state has the most lighthouses?"

"Well, California has a lot of shoreline," Lydia said.

"And Florida is almost all coast," Albert said.

"Where do you look up that sort of thing?" Lydia posed.

James and Bea approached Lydia and Albert.

"Hi!" James started. "How do you like this latest clue? I think they're getting harder all the time. How are we supposed to find this stuff out?"

"If it were too easy it wouldn't be as much fun," I whispered.

"So," began James. "Where do we start?"

"We go on shore at the Island of Little Current. Maybe we can ask a tour guide." I mentioned.

"Do you think they would know? Little Current is part of Ontario and the question is for the United States," James said.

"You'd be surprised how much more Canadians know about the U.S. than we do about Canada," I said.

"Now that I can believe. I get a Canadian television station at home and sometimes watch Canadian TV. One comedy spoofs Americans by going around asking them the dumbest questions like who is the King of Canada. Americans are stumped every time," James said.

"It's sad but true. Canadians know more about us than we know about them," James maintained.

"Agreed. So it stands to reason that this American doesn't know which state has the most lighthouses and how many and I'm willing to bet that some Canadian on the Island of Little Current does." I was anxious to figure out the clue.

"It won't hurt to ask around." James seemed to enjoy the scavenger hunt too.

Within the hour we docked at Little Current and were allowed to get off the ship. Almost everyone wanted to see the sights.

When we stepped off the boat it was like stepping back in time. There was a general store with a wooden floor so old it was warped. It carried penny candy and cloth and flour and all sorts of things. It wasn't a tourist trap. Some people relied upon the store.

I noticed a young clerk beside the register. I asked if she had any books on lighthouses. She pointed to a display rack that was littered with postcards and a few travel guides. I looked through one about Michigan. I skimmed it but I was too slow. I decided to buy the book on the off chance that I could find out who had the most lighthouses. Besides, I wanted the book anyway.

James was doing his own detective work. He asked a stock boy about lighthouses. The kid had no idea. He said he heard that as a trivia question on a radio station once but that he wasn't paying attention.

We left the general store and walked across to the ice cream parlor. I ordered a black cow, which is root beer and vanilla ice cream. James sat with me and just got a scoop of chocolate ice cream.

After, we walked around. James had his camera ready and was

shooting lots of pictures. The island was once used during the times of fur trading which dates back to the sixteen hundreds. This place had a real history.

The hub of the town was small and we were able to walk from one end to the other in about five minutes and that includes stops in between. But Amanda announced that we'd have a chance to hike around the island and spend our day that way.

James and I started out with the main group and tourist guide to get a feel for the history and lay of the land. But we'd sneaked away every chance we'd get to get that extra special photograph.

The red maples were splendid. The oaks burned yellow. Some orange color was in the background too. The trail was paved with leaves as if to lead us to our destination.

Even though James and I stole away at every chance, we stayed within constant earshot of the guide. This was no time to get lost.

James and I took off with the guide nearby and found a waterfall. The streaming water with the autumn background was gorgeous. First James took a picture with me in front of the falls. Then he began to take several pictures of the waterfall. He got one shot from the top of a hill. The grouping of trees just opened wide enough so that they encircled the waterfall. It was both delicate and powerful, the way only a waterfall can be.

We got closer to the waterfall for other shots. The sound of the rushing water was steady and like a siren's song, calling us closer in to explore.

And not unlike a siren, it wasn't too long before we had lost the group and were in the middle of the island with no idea how to get back.

"The good news is the ship won't take off without us. The bad news is we're lost." James wasn't happy to share that bit of news.

"Why didn't we bring a compass and a whistle?" I moaned.

"What did you say?" James asked.

"You heard me. Why are we lost without anything to help us find our way back?"

"That idea of a whistle is a great one. Let's call out. I'm not too proud. Let's call out for help as we try to retrace our steps," James suggested.

"Help!" I said in a meek little voice.

"That won't do you any good," James moaned.

"HELLO! CAN ANYONE HEAR US?"

We kept walking and clapping our hands and shouting. We'd listen. Just the sound of the waterfall in the distance was all we could hear.

"Let's mark the trail," James suggested.

"What do you mean?"

"We don't want to walk around in circles. I don't plan on staying lost for long. Make markings on trees by bending a branch at eye level. That way if we pass this way again we'll know we aren't getting anywhere," James instructed.

"Okay." I wasn't all that happy with our situation but I felt safe with James.

I noticed that below our feet the trail of leaves looked worn where we had walked. I suggested that we go were the leaves were scattered by footsteps and follow that. We did. We found ourselves back where we lost the group. But the group was gone. Now what?

We followed their trail of leaves some more and kept shouting. We also kept listening. Eventually we heard the group and were able to catch up.

I looked skyward and said thank you.

James was jovial when we caught up with the group. He wasn't embarrassed. He simply said, "You guys missed a beautiful waterfall."

The guide walked up to us. "I'm glad you decided to rejoin the group. It's not that big of an island but as you well know, it's possible to lose your way."

I didn't say much but Lydia came up to me and greeted me with, "You sure are brave."

"No, just stupid," I said. "I would have been scared except for James."

"You have quite the adventurous spirit. This place is scenic but full of all sorts of wildlife. I would have been afraid. What if a bear came up to you?" Lydia questioned me gently but with concern.

"My God! I never thought of that. Thank goodness we're back with the group. I can see it now…I fall down a hill and a pack of wild wolves decides to devour me. Yikes!" My hands started shaking. I guess the fear was just starting to catch up to me.

I continued, "I hope we didn't cut your walk short. I hope you didn't waste this gorgeous day looking for us."

Lydia remarked, "No honey, we didn't even notice you were gone until we heard your shouts and clapping. We had completed our tour. The important thing is that you are safe. I guess you had quite the hike yourself. James doesn't seem the least bit upset that he lost track of the group. I heard him bragging to Albert that he got a beautiful shot of a waterfall."

"You should have seen it. Now that I'm back safe from harm's way I can say it was worth it. It was as if the waterfall was just waiting for us to discover it. The colorful leaves and crisp air surrounding the scene set the tone. It doesn't get much better than this." I was happy to share my adventure with Lydia.

I saw James with a huge smile on his face as he showed the digital shots of his photos to Albert. Albert smiled too. There was no denying it—they were good photographs.

The group was getting ready to head back to the ship. No one seemed really upset with us that we were temporarily separated from the group. I still thank God that I didn't realize the trouble we could have gotten into until I talked to Lydia in the comfort of the group far from any danger.

James approached me and smiled. "I think our tour was better than their tour."

"I agree but next time count me out. Wolves or bears could have attacked us."

James laughed. Then he saw I was serious and stopped. "Don't worry. That won't happen again. No photograph is worth getting you that upset."

"Thank you. Now, let me see how it turned out. Where is the

digital image?"

"This one is my favorite." Jack pointed to a picture of the water-fall surrounded by fall color.

"It's a keeper," I smiled.

Chapter Eleven

"Roast duckling for the lady. Here are two quail for the gentleman. Enjoy!"

Dinner conversation was short and sweet: "This is delicious!" We didn't talk too much after that. Instead you could hear gurgles of contentment.

I finally came up for air.

"I take it you liked the duck." James was still trying to get every ounce of quail off the bones.

"And it looks like you're enjoying the quail."

The wine steward came by and asked how we enjoyed the wine he selected for our meal.

James remarked that he found it hard to believe that such a subtle wine came from a Michigan winery.

"Most of the wine we serve on this cruise is right here from Michigan. Many passengers marvel that local vintners can produce such fine quality wine. The bottle your drinking now is from the Old Mission Peninsula on the northwest coast of Michigan." The waiter said. "It's called 'Old Mission Cellars' and even though the color of your wine is clear, as if it were from a grape, it is actually produced from a cherry. The area is known for its temperate climate, which makes it a great place to produce wine."

"I didn't know a glass of wine had such a detailed history," I remarked.

The dining room held all the passengers at one sitting. Some tables held two, such as the one where James and I ate. Other tables held six or more. Lydia and Albert were at the Captain's Table tonight. I could hear Lydia laughing every now and then and I was sure she was having a great time.

The dining room had wood paneling in rich tones of a honey-colored hardwood. I got the feeling I was in an elite club. And I was. The food and wine were superb. The company was casual and refined. I knew I could mention the artwork of Botticelli and get an educated earful or I could ask about which ducks were indigenous to the area and I would also get an educated earful. This is a remarkable group.

Not being particularly interested in Botticelli or indigenous ducks, I was glad that James was by my side to keep me company.

"Want to hear a secret?" James whispered.

"Sure!" I said enthusiastically.

"I...um, I...um ah...I."

"You what?"

"I think you're special," James smiled.

I just blushed and then I said, "I knew I would have fun on this trip. What I didn't know is just how much fun. You have made this trip exciting. 'Special' doesn't begin to do you justice."

"That's one reason why I like you so much." James enjoyed the kind sentiments.

"You don't know how sweet it is to hear those words." I liked the kind sentiments too.

"And you are oblivious to your appeal. That's part of your charm," James grinned.

James kissed me right there on the spot.

"I don't want to rush into anything," I whispered.

"It's because I like you so much that I'm not rushing things. Do you get it?"

"I get it. And thank you." I felt calm. I felt safe. And I felt a little bit excited.

Immediately after that exchange I scooted my chair closer to James. I tried to use my softest husky voice but that didn't work.

Then I relaxed. Forget pretense. This is too much fun! Laughter came naturally to me because James has such a great sense of humor. I think I only heard about half of what he said because I kept feeling so lucky to be with this wonderful, handsome man. He is so attentive and mature without being bossy. This is a memory for the time capsule. I wanted to capture it like a firefly and preserve it forever.

Just because I stopped eating first doesn't mean I cleaned my plate. I couldn't finish my duck and that was a shame because it tasted so good. James polished off his quail with no problem. The cherry wine was delicious. It wasn't too sweet. I wouldn't know a "subtle" wine (the way James described it) from a "loud" wine (if there were such a thing. For a "loud" wine I conjured up an image of a Boone's Farm Wine). I just know it tasted good.

The dessert table rolled by us just slowly enough for us to ogle the gorgeous dishes and push ourselves back away from the table.

"Let's take a walk on the deck." James got up from the table and took my hand.

James led me out to the moonlight. The air had a snap to it. Fortunately, James took off his jacket and let me wear it.

I put my arms up around his neck and the sleeves still draped over my hands.

James kissed me gently. Then he took my hands in his as if to warm them up. Instead he put them next to his heart and said, "As I roam on these inland seas, I am discovering the beauty of the Great Lakes. That is plenty for a good vacation. But I've stumbled across something else…"

My heart was pounding a little when all of a sudden I heard Lydia say, "Oh aren't they a cute couple, Albert?"

Albert nodded. "Nice night for a moonlight stroll." He spoke quietly but not shyly.

James just smiled in agreement and they strolled one way and we strolled another. I'm glad it was a large boat. We wanted our space. That's what was so nice about this ship. Even though the cruise was booked it wasn't hard to find a private spot. New and old couples alike enjoyed that aspect.

"You know what's so great about this cruise?" James asked.

"Besides you?" I wondered.

"We're stuck on this boat. I guess to a claustrophobic that would be an awful feeling. The way I look at it, there is a freedom in accepting we're going where the boat takes us. It lets us surrender to having fun." James spoke quietly.

"I'm not fighting having fun. There is no surrender from me. I am here deliberately, consciously having fun," I added.

"No, it doesn't work that way. You don't deliberately, consciously have fun. Either it happens or it doesn't. But generally, you can't plan to create a memory. Instead, the right combination of elements comes together and voila, you have fun. It's more like magic than mind over matter."

"I think attitude has a lot to do with it," I said.

"Oh sure. I agree. I'm just saying those golden moments that stick with us as warm spots inside our hearts aren't always the meticulously planned moments but the quirky times we were caught off guard and pleasantly surprised. That's what makes those fluffy memories we store in a box to be recreated in our old age." James seemed to make good sense to me.

"This is a golden moment for me," I whispered.

"For me too." He was barely audible.

BAM!

"What the hell was that?" James rushed toward the noise.

I followed closely behind him.

Suddenly James burst out laughing. Evidently Albert had been drinking more than just a little cherry wine and fell into a lifeboat.

Albert wasn't laughing at first but then he burst into a loud roar. Lydia hid her giggles until she heard Albert laugh and then she couldn't hold back any longer.

By this point in time some others rushed over to see what the noise was all about. James showed his valor by not revealing that Albert was drunk. James spoke, not Albert, and said that a north wind had gusted just as Albert was looking into the small craft.

That seemed to satisfy the small gathering of curious people. They quickly left to set about their own moonlight walks on deck.

Albert had only been a little tipsy and was more than a little embarrassed that he had caused a scene.

Correction: James covered up for Albert and Albert was grateful. Albert is always so meticulous in his grooming and articulate with his language, so cunning with his bridge plays that this clumsy act was out of character.

But, in front of friends Albert didn't object to letting his guard down. He was having fun. He just was the type who liked to keep up appearances. Albert didn't want to hurt his flawless reputation.

Once everyone was gone, we all burst out laughing again.

"At least you didn't get hurt," James said.

"I guess I'm lucky," Albert said. "That cherry wine kind of sneaked up on me."

"Don't worry about a thing." Lydia spoke soothingly. "We're the only ones who know the real story. It's no big deal."

"You have to admit," Albert laughed. "It is sort of funny."

"I'm just glad you're okay," I said.

"Oh I'm more than okay at the moment. Ask me again tomorrow morning." Albert said.

The couple sauntered off and James and I were alone together again. We headed toward the direction of my cabin.

"Is your roommate in?" James asked.

"I don't know."

James gave me a long, passionate and tender kiss. I felt butterflies in my stomach. I squirmed a little and said I had to go inside.

Once alone and inside, I pulled out my journal and wrote:

"Is love in the air? Am I so swept away by the gorgeous scenery that life here looks prettier, and feels cheerier, seems brighter and appears better? Can I trust my heart that James is a truly nice guy? Can I allow myself to fall for a man when we're only spending a week together? Admittedly, it's some special week. Can I allow myself to MISS this opportunity?"

I got ready for bed and still pondered my situation. I am very shy and nervous when it comes to dating. Do I want to talk myself out of an exciting opportunity? I've spent more time with James on this cruise than I have with men I've dated for a long time. The timetable on board a cruise is different. It's kind of like counting in dog years. Every day equals a month here. We see each other constantly. We're certainly friends. Actually, I'd like to think there's more to it than a simple friendship. We're like peanut butter and chocolate. Each is fine alone but the combination is excellent.

I reached for the light by my bed to turn it out when I noticed the lighthouse book I had purchased before. I thumbed through it and discovered that Michigan is the state with the most lighthouses, followed by Maine. I'd have to tell James first thing in the morning. That only answered part of the question for the scavenger hunt. How MANY lighthouses does Michigan have? I'd have to figure out a way to get to that answer.

Chapter Twelve

When I got up in the morning, we were at Sault Ste. Marie. Soon we would be able to see the Soo Locks. If this is Day Five, these must be the Soo Locks.

The Soo Locks enabled shipping to expand to Lake Superior. Most of the cargo was iron ore but other items transported included coal and grain. They are among the largest locks in the world and also among the busiest. We would go through them twice…once to reach Lake Superior and another time to leave the biggest of the Great Lakes and get back onto Lake Huron.

For the moment the ship had thrown down her anchor in Lake Huron while the Captain checked up on the conditions at Lake Superior.

After my ritual of walking around the deck for exercise I could hardly wait to tell James that Michigan has the most lighthouses. When I did tell him he said that it made perfect sense. "Of course they are going to send us on fact-finding chases that highlight the Great Lakes," he reasoned.

Why didn't I think of that?

As James was talking I thought how comfortable I feel around him. He's like a teddy bear. He's soft and cuddly and I always have a warm feeling when he's around.

James is a gentle tease. I love a man with a sense of humor. I don't think putting other people down especially shows quick wit. To me it shows little patience. James liked most people. He didn't denigrate them for the sake of a joke.

We're alike enough so that we don't argue but different enough so that I can't predict his next move. I never really know what to expect from James.

I was just about to compliment him lavishly when I heard the cry, "Man overboard!"

"Oh my God!" I shouted.

James got up and I followed. We looked over the rail of the deck and saw someone down in the chilly water below. It was a young man, college-aged, oiled up with long swim trunks and swim goggles on. In other words, he went in intentionally. What he didn't bargain for was just how cold the water would be. He tried to grab the life preserver thrown to him but his body was cramping up.

The crew called the Coast Guard. The Coast Guard was there within minutes. The man was hoisted up to the Coast Guard tug and they immediately put towels around him.

"What in the world were you thinking?" Captain Bill asked.

The young man's brother spoke up. "My brother and I made this bet that we could get Cruise Director Amanda's attention if one of us jumped over. Bob jumped and I yelled, 'man overboard' so that he would be saved immediately. It serves him right because he kept bragging that Amanda liked him more than she likes me. I wonder how she feels now."

"That is one of the dumbest things I've ever heard!" the Captain shouted. "That sort of prank might be tolerated at a fraternity but it's forbidden here. You could have been killed!"

Bob still hadn't grasped the gravity of the situation. He was shivering and dripping wet but he was grinning. Even his brother let out a laugh.

The boisterous boys with bravado soon got a crash course in reality.

Once Bob, the brother who dived in, was back on board the Captain said that he would have to be accompanied by a crew member at all times he was not in his cabin. The captain stressed this was not a joke.

Bob was hoping that Amanda would be the crewmember assigned to him. He didn't seem a bit phased by the Captain's punishment. In fact, he grinned at that thought.

"I don't think you'll be smirking for long," the Captain said. "Yule!" Captain Bill yelled. A hefty and hairy maintenance worker looked up.

"I hate to do this to you, Yule, but I need you to watch these characters every moment of the cruise." The Captain was not about to reward foolishness.

Captain Bill continued, "It looks to me as if you proven that you don't have your head on straight. That means if you so much as want to walk out of your room you'll have to call from your cabin and make arrangements with Yule."

Bob's head dropped down to his chest. He thought he was proving his virility when instead he came off like a fool.

The ship's doctor got a look at the Bob and reported that Bob seemed just fine. He was a little cold but all he needed was a warm drink and to dry off his soaked and chilled body.

Bob couldn't have been more disappointed. Yule threw out his cigarette over the deck and began to follow a blanketed Bob and his brother, Nathan, to their cabin.

"Why did you rat me out?" Bob asked his brother Nathan.

"Did you see how mad the Captain was? I had no choice," Nathan answered.

The three guys disappeared but the Coast Guard was still there and just getting ready to leave.

With the Coast Guard so handy I couldn't resist asking one of the men how many lighthouses are in the state of Michigan.

"Why do you plan to jump overboard and swim to one?" he asked.

"No, we've got this scavenger hunt going and I'm trying to solve the clues," I mumbled.

"Until the 1990's, Michigan had seen the construction of 90 lighthouses in its history. Maine follows with about 80. But it depends what you count as a lighthouse. I figure the answer could be as high as 130. Right now there are about 96 working lighthouses." He rattled off the statistics like a computer.

I was grateful for the information. I still wasn't sure which number was the answer to my clue.

I wrote down what the Coast Guard fellow said. I figured he had to be right because he gave three numbers in one answer. One of them had to be what Amanda was wanted.

We made our way through the Soo Locks without incident. No one jumped off the ship. But nearly everyone crowded around the railing to watch the locks at work.

The ship before us carried iron ore. It was a big freighter and it took some time for the big barge to get through.

Then it was our turn. We were in the lower waters of Lake Huron so once in the locks the water needed to be elevated to the higher waters of Lake Superior.

Once we were through we saw the pristine waters of the largest of the Great Lakes. Lake Superior covers an area of 31,400 square miles. It is 355 miles in length and the average depth is about 1000 feet.

As we were safely on Lake Superior, Captain Bill told tales of ships who didn't survive the gales on Lake Superior. Most famous of all was The Wreck of the Edmund Fitzgerald known from Gordon Lightfoot's ballad. In his song, Lightfoot poetically describes how the American ship came back from a mill in Wisconsin, loaded and heading for Cleveland. Of the more than 1000 ships that have sunk in the Great Lakes, the Fitzgerald is the largest to ever go down. She weighed 13,632 tons and was 729 feet long by 75 feet wide. Fully loaded, she was able to carry 27,500 tons. A boat rides high in the water when it is empty and low in the sea when she is full. The ship had a 7,500 horsepower steam turbine engine that could move her to speeds up to 20 mph. In 1964 the Fitzgerald was the first carrier to carry over one million tons of iron ore pellets known as taconite through the locks at Sault Ste. Marie. That feat gave her the nickname "Big Fitz" or "The Pride of the American Flag." She was bigger than most freighters and the largest carrier on the Great Lakes until 1971.

The captain, Ernest McSorely, had over 40 years of experience. Members of the crew considered it an honor to serve aboard the Fitzgerald.

The boat was traveling along side of the Arthur Anderson when a storm approached them. Ten-foot waves started as early as 1 a.m. November 10. The gale was upgraded to a storm warning and the waves reached from eight to 15 feet. The storm raged on. The Fitzgerald was taking on water. By 4 p.m. that day, hurricane-force winds hit and McSorely wired the ship Anderson that the boat had lost both her radars. He asked the Anderson to guide him. The gusting wind also knocked out the lighthouse at Whitefish Point along with its radio. At 5:45 McSorely wired to the ship the Avafors that the Fitzgerald was suffering in "one of the worst seas I've ever seen." At 7:15 p.m., November 10, the Anderson lost the Fitzgerald on its radar screen and a snow squall had developed.

On November 10, 1975, the entire crew of 29 men was lost at sea with the sinking of the Edmund Fitzgerald. It sank 17 miles north-northwest of Whitefish Point, Michigan. As is said in Lightfoot's ballad, "Superior, they said, never gives up her dead when the gales of November come early!"

Whitefish Point is home of the Great Lakes Shipwreck Museum. The Great Lakes Shipwreck Historical Society sent three underwater expeditions to the wreck in 1989, 1994, and in 1995. It was the 1995 dive when they recovered the 200 lb. Bronze bell which is now on display in the Great Lakes Shipwreck Museum as a tribute to her lost crew. The diving team sent down a replica of the bronze bell to the wreck with all the crewmembers' names on it replacing the recovered bronze bell.

Old Mariners' Church of Detroit is possibly the reason the shipwreck got so much attention. The Reverend Richard Ingalls was Rector at Old Mariners' at the time of the Fitzgerald's sinking. It was Ingalls who prayed for the crew. On November 11 he rang the church bell 29 times, once for each member that was lost in the sinking. The media got wind of this memorial and soon the Edmund Fitzgerald and the Mariners' Church of Detroit were famous.

The Old Mariner's Church of Detroit was established back in 1842. Ingalls, the man who first paid his respects to those lost from the Edmund Fitzgerald, is still the Rector at the Old Mariner's Church today. Captain Bill told the story with such detail it felt as if I could see his descriptions. The crowd listening was totally silent. When the captain finished the group stayed silent for about a minute and then began its normal hum of activity.

The day was so gorgeous we didn't think about shipwrecks or cold and blustery days. Instead, blue is the best word I can think of to describe this event. A gorgeous blue sky met the horizon of deep blue waters. And while the wind from the lake made it a little bit chilly, the brilliant hues of blues made the location seem like heaven on earth.

The sun shone brightly giving us visibility of about ten miles. We felt as if we were let in on a little known secret. The hush of the wild shoreline almost spoke to us. This was no ordinary trip.

Someone spotted an eagle flying overhead.

Folks who came to see the Soo Locks stayed for seeing Lake Superior. There was no comparison between a marvel of modern man and the majesty of nature.

Barely anyone spoke. We soaked up the silence as if it were magic. The tonic of fresh air surrounded by fresh water seemed to have the effect of making everyone calm…and a little bit reverent.

Eventually the cool breeze from the lake won and most people went back to their cabins to get a sweater or jacket or just to warm up.

Amanda announced over the loudspeaker that we would be celebrating Oktoberfest tonight. "Be sure to bring your appetite and get ready for some fun."

The celebration started around five p.m. A folk band had assembled with men dressed in Bavarian garb of lederhosen. One man played the accordion.

The ship's staff brought out plates of sausage and rolls. The women wait staff wore dirndls and carried mugs of beer.

As the accordion player cranked out the old tunes the rest of the band danced traditional folk dances from Germany. It was a lot of fun.

We ate our sausage and drank our beer and laughed as we watched.

Lydia and Albert sat next to James and me. Albert told the story about how he was in Munich during a real Oktoberfest. He said the place was covered with huge tents. Inside the tents nearly every long table was filled with drinkers. He said many of the people at the festival were not German but tourists. He said a lot of military men on leave were there.

Albert described how the waitresses carried six two-liter glasses of beer, three in each hand. They did it with expertise and no signs of fatigue.

With Albert's stories there's always a touch of the unexpected. Albert said he visited that festival when he was still in college and studying abroad.

Despite warnings from professors at his school, people who knew the ropes around Europe and festivals, Albert and a group from his study program went to Munich without hotel reservations.

"We were young. We thought, 'How many other people could there be?'" Albert asked.

He went on to say that there were thousands of people at the Oktoberfest and that he and most of his group ended up sleeping on the cold floor of the train station. One woman in their group said she was glad her mother couldn't see her then.

A group of Eastern Europeans also sat at the train station and they laughed as the Americans stretched out for the night.

"I guess it's a good thing we had consumed plenty of beer. I don't think we would have had the nerve to do that otherwise." Albert laughed as he told the story. "We make so many mistakes when we are young and yet sometimes those memories are the happiest."

"I think it takes courage to make a mistake," James announced. "Being right all the time is so dull. How can you expect to learn anything?

It does us good to stretch a little. I remember my mistakes more vividly than I remember when something was a cinch for me."

"That's true," I said. "As long as the experience isn't humiliating. I long remember embarrassing moments but still wish they hadn't happened."

Albert piped in, "No, don't you see? Those are the times we look back on and laugh. You aren't born knowing how to do everything perfectly. It's trial and error. You might as well accept that and have some fun with it."

Lydia looked at me and said, "Let the boys make the mistakes...don't you think?"

"Oh everybody makes mistakes," James groaned. "I think Albert and I get over it faster because we aren't as upset at the thought of looking foolish."

"Speaking of looking foolish...look who has a crew member by his side," Albert mentioned.

We all looked up and there was Bob, the man who jumped overboard.

We all just laughed.

"Now that took guts!" James said.

"Or stupidity," Lydia added.

"He sure won't forget this trip," Albert concluded.

"Let's drink to the man who had the courage to make a mistake!" James exclaimed.

We all lifted our glasses. The beer kept flowing. Albert was cautious not to drink too much. Lydia and I never really drank seriously. And James seemed so calm and easygoing it's hard to tell if he's had a few drinks or not. I'm glad. At least he wasn't a rowdy drinker.

Eventually people from the cruise got up to dance. They didn't exactly polka. They didn't exactly do folk dances. They hopped around to the beat of the music. While each might not have had the steps down perfectly, every dancer displayed a happy countenance. It was infectious. Before I knew it I was on the other side of James, sometimes my hands were slapping my thighs and other times my hands were clapping James' hands. I had no idea what I was doing but it was fun.

Lydia and Albert looked equally ridiculous. I guess it was a good thing we had that talk about looking foolish. That didn't seem to matter one ounce right now. Fun trumped self-consciousness.

Who knows how long we lasted on deck jumping up and down to beer-barreled music? Time flew so I can't tell you how long we were there except that the sun started to set. The horizon was ablaze with reddish orange and the deep shade of blue of the water seemed a shade of cobalt blue.

We didn't notice the weather but storm clouds had started to form. The captain saw this right away. He ordered the band to stop playing and for everyone to get off the deck and into their cabins or in the dining room.

The Captain maneuvered the boat to the safety of a cove where we would wait until the storm passed over.

Being stuck in a storm on Lake Superior is about the last thing anyone would want. Remembering the recent recital of shipwrecks, I did not want to be among them.

James and I went to the dining room. We heard the rain falling and felt the boat rock because of the waves beneath her. This wasn't in the brochure.

One hand firmly grabbed the table in front of me while my other hand took a hold of James.

"It'll be okay," he reassured me.

We peeked out the portholes and saw rain coming down sideways because of the wind.

The captain announced that we were in a small squall but that we were in no danger. He had dropped anchor close to shore and out of harm's way.

"We can sit through this with white knuckles," James said. "Or we can enjoy ourselves. How about it? Are you up for a game of cribbage?"

I reluctantly said yes. I kept making little comments like it's a good thing the pegs are in the holes in the cribbage board or they would fall out in this rocky weather.

James ignored me. He did worse than that—he skunked me. That made me just mad enough to forget about the storm and to demand the best two out of three.

By the time we were done with our third game of cribbage, (I won one; James won two) the storm was over.

Night had fallen. The bad weather had ceased. So James and I decided to go back up on deck to look at the stars. You've never seen a night sky until you are in the middle of Lake Superior. The sky was aglow with more stars than I thought were possible.

"I see Orion. See? There's his belt," James pointed.

"I'm still looking for the Big Dipper." I squinted my eyes to see the stars better.

James stood behind me and wrapped his arms around me. He held my arm and pointed up as he said, "There it is. See?"

The sky was spectacular. I wondered what the stars held in store for us.

Chapter Thirteen

I woke up happy. That's not to say that I usually wake up sad. It's that I woke up cheerier than usual.

Today we are going to see Mackinac Island. I had been there once as a little girl but that was a long time ago. It's Day Six of our cruise.

Before we left the boat Amanda told us the Legend of the origin of Mackinac Island.

It went like this:

A woman, who was a spirit, lived high in the sky. She was lonely so she asked Kitche Manitou, The Great Spirit, to send her a companion. The Great Spirit obliged. Because of her companion the sky woman conceived two children: one of the earth, one of the sky. Since the two were opposites they fought until they both died.

The sky woman was alone again. The Great Spirit sent her another companion who also left her.

The creatures of the water saw this and felt sorry for the sky woman. The creatures of the water asked a giant turtle to emerge from the lake and allow the sky woman to stay on his back. The water creatures then asked the sky woman to come down. She did.

When she arrived she asked the animals of the water to get her some soil from the bottom of the lake. The beaver tried and had no luck. The marten tried with the same re-

sults. The loon tried and was as unsuccessful as the other water creatures. They wanted to help the sky woman but they were not able.

The muskrat, overlooked and scorned, asked if he might try to get soil form the bottom of the lake. He dived down and was gone a very long time. The other creatures worried about the muskrat because he was down in the water for so long.

After much waiting the muskrat reached the water's surface with a small bit of soil from the bottom of the lake. The animals of the water nurtured the sick muskrat while the sky woman painted the back of the turtle with the soil. Since she was a spirit of the sky, she was able to breathe life into the soil and she created an island.

The turtle's job was done so he swam away but the island remained.

The island the sky woman created was called Mishee Mackinakong, the Ojibway name that means place of the turtle's back. They also called the island Michilimackinac or Mackinac Island.

And so goes the Ojibway (or Ojibwa) version of the Mackinac Island legend.

Mackinac Island is shaped like a turtle's back so the legend proved interesting. While we weren't about to encounter any sky spirits, every single passenger was anxious to see Mackinac Island. It is a place filled with charm.

We were just about to leave the ship when Amanda gave us another Scavenger Hunt clue. It read:

On this island a movie was made
Starring a Superman.
Tell the name of this love story
If you think you can.

We all left the boat. I noticed that Lydia and Albert were smiling. I think they already knew the answer to the clue.

James and I looked around the quaint summer resort of Mackinac. It had Victorian houses and shops. Fudge was a big seller there. People who lived on the island called tourists "fudgies."

No cars are allowed on the island so we had three choices: walk, rent a bike, or take a horse-drawn carriage.

James and I elected to walk but we saw many of the ship's passengers get into a horse-drawn buggy.

Walking gave us a chance to see the wonderfully restored homes that now served as B & B's or shops. We did get some fudge and it was the best I've ever had.

Our goal was to reach the Grand Hotel. The Grand Hotel is world famous and overlooks the Straits of Mackinac. Its porch is the longest summer porch in the world. Back when travel was mostly by trains and boats, the Grand Hotel was a favorite destination for many. It still is.

James got a beer and I got a glass of lemonade. We seated ourselves on the vast porch.

The view was spectacular. The grounds before us were immaculate. But the real scene-stealer was the waterway in front us. We watched ships and sailboats and tugs going past us. You name a watercraft and we saw it. James was relaxed but he also got out his camera and shot pictures. His trained eye saw new ways to capture the beauty in front of us. He might have a tree with turning leaves in the corner of the foreground. He took a wide-angle picture of the porch of the hotel making it look even bigger than it actually is.

We sat on the porch quite a while. James was content with his beer and I kept ordering glasses of lemonade. We didn't notice how much time we spent on the porch. Time flew by. Were we there an hour, or half the day? We didn't know. But also we felt a connection to days gone to around 1887, the time the hotel was built. It didn't take too much effort to imagine women in long dresses with their hair in the Gibson-girl fashion and gentlemen dressed in white suits carrying pocket watches but having no need to look at them at this enchanted outpost.

As I sat there thinking about how time had stopped for us, it came to me.

"I've got it!" I yelled to James.

"What are you talking about?"

"The answer for the Scavenger Hunt. The movie filmed here was called "Somewhere in Time." Did you ever see it?"

"No. It sounds like a chick flick."

"Oh no, it's a beautiful movie. It's about true love," I exclaimed.

I found Amanda and told her the name of the movie. She smiled and said that so far James and I were ahead in the Scavenger Hunt.

James walked up behind me and asked how Lydia and Albert were doing with the hunt.

"They are the only ones even close to you," Amanda commented.

After James and I finally pulled ourselves away from the hypnotic appeal of the view from the porch of the Grand Hotel, and after we had checked in with Amanda, we walked into town to get an ice cream.

James saw a horse and buggy and insisted we take a ride. I loved it. The horse and guide took us through the narrow streets and down Main Street. It really did feel as if we were in a bygone time. James clicked photos of some of the appealing Victorian homes.

With no cars on the island life was tranquil and yet everywhere you looked people were busy talking, eating, exploring, and enjoying. It really was like stepping back in time.

Amanda gathered us all together to get back on board. We were to see Lake Michigan.

Then it would be time to turn around and head home. That thought saddened me.

* * * * *

Once we were back on board Captain Bill made the announcement that Lake Michigan is the third largest of the Great Lakes measuring 22,400 square miles. He said it was about 340 miles long and the average depth was nearly 990 feet. He also said the state of Michigan has over 31,000 miles of shoreline. He pointed out that Michigan's shoreline is longer than the entire Atlantic seaboard of the United States!

People nodded as the Captain spoke. It's one thing to read about a place or adventure. It's another thing to experience it. Having traveled all five of the Great Lakes we could appreciate the Captain's statistics. Amanda then spoke up and gave us our next clue:

> *The legend of Mackinac*
> *Dealt with a woman who came from the sky.*
> *Tell the Legend of the Sleeping Bear Dunes,*
> *How they got their name and why.*

"Where in the world are we going to find the solution to that clue?" Lydia asked. I wasn't so sure where I'd find the answer either.

Lots of people shrugged their shoulders when they heard this clue.

Instead of saying, "Is there a doctor in the house?" Someone said, "Is there a teacher aboard?"

I didn't speak up.

Lake Michigan is the lake furthest away from the St. Lawrence Seaway. As a result, it takes the longest amount of time for this lake to cleanse itself. And yet it glimmered with beauty.

The air wasn't quite as cold as when we were on Lake Superior.

Today some skeet shooters had the crew pull clay pigeons. The sight and sounds of sea gulls usually surrounded our ship. Not today. Not any day when skeet shooters were practicing. This was a cruise for all tastes.

This was also a busy day. First we spent time on Mackinac Island and now Lake Michigan. When we finally saw the Sleeping Bear Dunes most people got out their cameras. The sky just had a whisper or two of a white cloud in it. The water was a brilliant and shimmering greenish blue. The vast area of sand dunes seemed to go on without end. We saw some whitecaps near the shore but for the most part the essence of the whole scene was calm. Every now and then we saw a sandbar with a pool of water toward the shoreline. Our ship passed a forest that had been buried by sand. Bare trees jutted out of the sand. Seeing how the dunes were so tall I wondered what it would be like to walk uphill in sand? I'm sure it's hard work.

Fortunately we didn't have to walk anywhere. We had the best seats in the house from the deck of our ship. Here footprints were as fleeting as the wind itself. Memories lasted much longer.

Dusk was coming. The gorgeous sunset held us captive until the sky was practically dark. The day was giving way to night.

I went to my cabin to get my camera and I noticed my roommate had a tour book of the Great Lakes. I looked inside and found the Legend of the Sleeping Bear Dunes.

According to this book, The Ojibway (sometimes called Chippewa or Ojibwa) legend said that long ago in a land that is now called Wisconsin, Mother Bear and her two cubs fled a raging forest fire. The cubs swam their best but the distance and the water were too much for them. They fell further behind until they slipped under the waves. When Mother Bear reached the Michigan shore, she climbed on top of a bluff and looked across the water, searching for her cubs. The Great Spirit took pity on her. He raised the North and South Manitou Islands to mark the spot where the cubs had disappeared and placed Mother Bear in a deep slumber where the dunes now stand.

I closed the book and wept for the Mother Bear. Don't ask me why.

Chapter Fourteen

Tonight was to be a big night. It was our last night on board the liner. It's funny how close you can get to people in such a short time. I had the good fortune of meeting great people right away. Their company was a treat. I would miss them.

Tonight is also a big night because it's the night of the costume party. I got dressed up as Little Miss Muffet so I wore a dress in the fashion of a young girl and affixed a dangling spider over my head.

I approached Amanda and told her I had discovered the Legend of the Sleeping Bear Dunes.

Amanda was very friendly stating that James and I were the frontrunners in the contest.

Tonight the excitement level was high. It was our last night and a lot of us would be going our separate ways very soon. Everyone planned on dressing up tonight in costumes for dinner and then dancing to the ship's band.

Some outfits showed a lot of thought. Others were simply funny.

I surveyed the room. Across from us sat the older women I had first seen in the hotel in Toronto. They were dressed as a giant version of M & M candies. One costume was red the other was green. They had gentlemen at their table. One older gent went as a pirate and had a fake parrot on his shoulder. The other was decked out as a Dapper Dan. He wore tails and a top hat. He even had spats. I could hear the sound of their laughter. Everyone seemed so happy.

I had to squint a bit to see them because they hid in a back corner, but I noticed the brothers, the infamous jumping-overboard brothers.

One had a round life preserver around his neck that read S.S. Minnow. The other was dressed in a Coast Guard uniform. I'm glad they were able to laugh at themselves. They were seated together along with Yule, the most distinguished member of that table. His job of watching the brothers was no cakewalk. And yet Yule showed the best sense of humor of all. He went as a ballerina. Yule wore a pink tutu and tights. He was the hairiest ballerina I've ever seen.

I saw my Lithuanian roommate and her German male friend. They looked happy dressed as Hansel and Gretel.

I saw many sets of older couples, obviously still very much in love with each other. It was heartwarming to see these couples hold hands or whisper in a mate's ear or know that the other's likes and tastes better than he or she knew them…no lemon on the fish…dressing is to be placed on the side…only sugar substitutes…these are the details of daily lives shared together. One table of the older set went as flappers and bootleggers. Women wore beaded drop waist dressed and the guys had pinstriped suits. One even carried a violin case.

You could tell who the seasoned seafarers were. Those who had been on cruises before were very prepared with great costumes. Others had to throw together what they could with what they had. It was a nice mix of the whimsical with the elegant.

A group of four that traveled together went as fruit. One man was a banana. His wife was a bunch of grapes. Another man went as an apple. His wife went as a strawberry.

One couple went together as a pair of Lipton Tea Bags. They wore the sacks that looked like tea around their bodies and each had a huge tag that read "Lipton" on it.

The Captain and crewmembers went as the cast of Love Boat. Captain Bill wore a skullcap that made him look partially bald. Now he looked just like Captain Merrill Stubing. Amanda curled her hair so she looked just like the Cruise Director Julie. The bartender had on a fake mustache and looked like Isaac. The ship's purser was a dead ringer for Gopher. The ship's doctor was bespectacled just for this occasion and he looked just like "Doc" from the show.

The crew's efforts weren't wasted. This is a crowd who had

been around long enough to remember the TV show Love Boat.

Lydia and Albert were dressed as the cards the King and Queen of Hearts. With Albert's love of bridge it wasn't a stretch for him to go dressed as a card.

James was pretending to be a National Geographic photographer on assignment. He wore a pith helmet and a khaki colored short sleeve shirt and khaki pants. He had a camera around his neck. It was a good thing too because he was able to take great pictures of this, one of the most colorful events of our trip.

We all enjoyed the trip. Most people were enjoying the moment too much to be sad that the fun was about to end.

James and Albert told the waiter to bring a bottle of champagne. I looked around at my last dinner aboard the boat.

The Captain's table was full, as usual, and Captain Bill was entertaining the seated guests with tales of his travels. I could hear the sound of laughter and applause from there.

The tuxedoed waiters seemed invisible until someone needed more water or dropped a fork. Then they would appear out of nowhere and be eager to please.

The band was seated at a table near the dance floor. The guys in the band looked like the Beatles from the St. Pepper's Album. The female vocalist looked like Marilyn Monroe in a low-cut beaded dress and platinum blonde wig.

When I heard the pop of the cork of the champagne bottle my attention returned swiftly to my table.

Albert seemed especially happy tonight. That surprised me because I knew he adored Lydia and this was their last night together.

Not so. Albert announced that he planned to visit Lydia in the near future. Lydia announced that she, in turn, planned to visit Albert. So for them it wasn't goodbye.

My heart sank a little. It would be goodbye for James and me. I kept telling myself to enjoy the moment.

I had rack of lamb. Lydia had pan-fried trout. James and Albert were more adventurous. James had boar stew. We could hardly wait until the dish arrived to see what was in it. It had boar, bacon, carrots, tomatoes, and potatoes—plus seasoning. Neither Lydia nor I wanted to taste it but we wanted to know what it tasted like. James and Albert both had a hard time describing the taste of their dishes. Albert had bear kabobs. The waiter told Albert that bear-meat is like pork in the sense that both meats have to be cooked through. Albert assured us that that's where the similarity ended. The bear kabobs looked ordinary enough. They had cherry tomatoes, green peppers, big mushrooms and onions. Albert said the bear tasted like nothing else he'd ever had. This next question still left Lydia and I in the dark but James asked Albert if the bear tasted gamier than venison. "Oh yes!" Albert said.

James remarked that the boar was gamier than venison too. Still, he didn't regret ordering it.

My rack of lamb tasted better with each description of the other meals. Bear? Boar?

We all agreed that we would try the gooseberry pie. James liked it so much he asked for the recipe. The waiter came back quickly with the list of ingredients (2 cups gooseberries, 1 ½ cup sugar, 1/8 tsp baking soda, 2 tbsp cornstarch, and pastry crust for a two-crust pie). The instructions said to heat the gooseberries and sugar. Put soda and cornstarch in a little water and mix in with the gooseberries. Bring to a boil. When heated add 1 tbsp butter and a dash of nutmeg. Put in the crust and bake at 425 for 35 to 45 minutes or until the crust is golden.

James nodded with understanding as he read the instructions. James takes stunning photos, he's easygoing, he likes to dance, he's charming, and he cooks! Of course I'm attracted to him!

When we finished eating, Amanda stood up and said she had an award or two to hand out. People became quiet at first and then they mumbled among themselves, speculating. Amanda then asked Lydia, Albert, James and me to come up to the microphone.

I figured we had tied with Lydia and Albert for the scavenger hunt and that was Amanda's reason for bringing all four of us up to the front. Instead, Amanda said that Lydia and Albert had the best costume of the party. They went as the King and Queen of Hearts.

Everyone knew Albert was a superb bridge player so *his* costume made sense. But Amanda asked Lydia how she came up with the Queen of Hearts costume when she had just met Albert on the cruise.

Lydia blushed and said, "Albert told me about his costume so we came up with the idea together. At one of the ports I got the materials I needed to match Albert. Albert did the artwork. He knows cards so well that drawing a realistic Queen of Hearts wasn't a stretch for him."

"Well," Amanda replied. "Your costumes won the prize. You each win one of these masks."

I looked up and saw that they were the kind of masks you hold up with one hand—the kind that the gentry used hundreds of years ago at parties or balls. They looked like something you might see at Mardi Gras. Lydia's mask was white while Albert's mask was black. It was hard enough to carry off elegance dressed as cards but they managed to make the costumes look refined. Now with these opera masks they looked like royalty at a dignitary's party.

Then Amanda turned to James and me. "I don't want to embarrass you two but you beat everyone else in the scavenger hunt by a landslide! And since you were the best sleuths, we decided this trophy made the best sense for you two." She handed us a little statue of Sherlock Holmes with his traditional hat holding a magnifying glass. The tiny magnifier was looking at an even tinier map of the Great Lakes.

James laughed at the statue and handed it to me. I clutched it and brought it to my body, completely forgetting that I was standing in front of a crowd. I was thrilled that we won.

Then a member of the crew stood up and said that since this was Captain Bill's last cruise on the Great Lakes they felt that it was appropriate to wish him well in a manner befitting the ship's captain.

I was expecting speeches. Instead, the crewmember hammed it up and said that before Captain Bill became a captain, he thought "port" was a wine, he thought "starboard" meant a cruise filled with celebrities, and the misguided captain thought that Seven Seas was a salad dressing. "Now," he said. "If you give Captain Bill an inch, he'll take a nautical mile." It ended with him saying, "In the flotsam and jetsam that clutters our lives, we wish you smooth sailing, especially you, Captain Bill, especially you."

Captain Bill stood up and thanked the speaker. He went on to say that everyone knows that Seven Seas IS a salad dressing and that he was pretty sure it was being served at this very dinner.

The Captain sat down and within minutes nearly everyone got up and danced. If you are willing to dress up as an M & M or a tea bag, you aren't self-conscious on the dance floor. I can't tell you how many times people asked me who I was. Once they saw my dangling spider and I said that I was Little Miss Muffet, they laughed. Sure I felt dumb but it also felt nice to be dancing with James.

The night flew by. It seemed as if just a minute ago I was on the dance floor for the first time. How could this possibly be the band's last dance?

I was lucky enough to dance with just about everyone, including the mischievous brothers, each of them. I also got to dance with Yule, the biggest, roundest ballerina on the planet. But every slow dance James came and found me. Those dances were just for us.

So where did the night go? How could it all be over so soon?

All I know was that suddenly I was back in my cabin with James. He kissed me. Yura was off with Hansel somewhere. If there were a time for us to be together, this was the moment.

James whispered in my ear, "I love you."

I whispered back, "Me too."

We fumbled in the darkness.

I felt awkward but James was in no rush and he gave me no reason to feel anything but cherished.

Chapter Fifteen

When I awoke, got the sleep out of my eyes, and remembered last night, my mind kept racing. Throughout the cruise James was wonderful. Still, seven days does not a true love make. Or does it? Is it possible to fall in love in a week? My mind was racing. This wasn't my style…to get cozy with a guy…to have a fling. But James was different. I cared about him. He seemed to care about me. What will become of us?

We felt such a connection last night. I can hardly wait to see him today. Do I dare ask where we go from here?

I'm not so sure I know that answer myself. What if he wants nothing to do with me now? Do I know him as well as I thought I did?

I wonder how he feels about me. I really wanted to tell him it was totally out of character for me to be with him last night. I wanted to tell him even more that he must be special for me to let my reserve down like that.

Did he care?

I kept mulling in my mind what life would be like back on shore. Would I see James again?

I finally got out of bed and began the routine of getting ready to greet the morning. What if I never see James again? Am I any worse off? Didn't he make my seven-day cruise spectacular?

It wasn't a casual fling for me but I can't expect him to be truly, madly, and deeply in love with me so suddenly. So where does that leave us? I'm almost afraid to approach him with all of these questions because what if he rejects me? What if he thinks that I'm a complete loon for wanting a relationship?

And what do I want? Do I know him well enough to see our future when I look in his eyes?

Stop! Get a grip! Okay, I might have made a mistake last night. I might have been carried away by the magic of the moment. I'm never casual about intimacy and this was not casual. I thought the two words together—"casual" and "intimacy"—make an oxymoron. But wasn't this my chance to fly? If not now, when?

It's not James I need to forgive. Should I forgive myself? Is what I did so wrong that I'll feel guilty for a long time to come? Or can I be honest with myself and say I was simply following my heart?

Or is my heart about to break because I put more stock into a relationship than James did?

I kept telling myself to be logical. I said to myself that this is a time to look at the facts: I'm no longer a telemarketer. That's good news. I don't have a job anymore. That's bad news. I'll get to tell Uncle Ned about all the beautiful places I saw, thanks to him. That's good news. I'll get to show off my pictures. Uncle Ned will especially love that because it's been a few years since he was on the lakes. That's terrific news! Even if James has nothing more to do with me after this trip, it was far from a waste.

There was a photo lab on board the ship so we could get most of our photos developed right there. I handed in my many rolls of film previously and I was very eager to see how they turned out.

Even though James had a digital camera, a small image on the back of a fancy camera is not the same as a glossy print in your hand. I wanted to see his photos too.

I had my bags all packed. I saw Yura, my Lithuanian roommate. We hugged each other goodbye and promised each other a postcard.

Soon we would be at Port Huron. I was in no rush to get home.

Once my baggage was taken care of I decided to go on deck and soak in the sights as best I could.

I took in a breath of sea air and then I went to the dining room for breakfast. Why am I feeling so low? Everyone else seems to be able to accept the fact that the cruise is almost over.

I barely touched my food. As delicious as I knew it was, I didn't have much of an appetite.

I noticed that the others came in and out of the dining room casually. They had their fun. Now it was time for everyday life.

I didn't see James anywhere. I wasn't about to hunt him down. Still, I was hoping to see him before we all went our separate ways.

I began my goodbye ritual. Ever since I was little, when I left a place that I truly loved I would say goodbye to each element of it. Somehow that made leaving easier.

So after breakfast I said, "Goodbye dining room."

I walked around the deck and said, "Goodbye deck."

I looked over the railing and said, "Goodbye Lake Huron. You are prettier than I ever imagined."

I looked out over the water and saw a barge and a few large sailboats. A lighthouse down the way was red and white. The seagulls surrounded our boat and squawked.

"Goodbye ships passing by. Goodbye seagulls."

I walked around the whole deck. This time I didn't do it for exercise. I did it to absorb as much as possible before it was time to leave.

I noticed that Yule, the crewmember assigned to Bob, was accompanying Bob and his brother, Nathan, off the boat. That made me smile. I thought, *Goodbye Bob, you fool. Goodbye Yule, you good sport.*

Then I saw James. He looked so handsome. I was about to approach him when he turned and saw me. He gave me a wave with his hand. He kept on walking without so much as saying the word "goodbye."

I felt very foolish. Obviously I didn't mean as much to James as he meant to me.

I picked up my developed photos from the trip. Of course I thought of James, Mr. Photographer, and how I would have loved to see how his pictures turned out. So much for THAT wish! I knew in my heart that I was wishing for more than just a glimpse of his snapshots.

I was wallowing in self-pity and I didn't even care. In the same way people indulge in a hot fudge sundae, I treated myself to a good pout.

I looked around and saw Lydia and Albert. They were just out of earshot so we all waved goodbye. Somehow their farewell didn't hurt me as much as James and his brush-off wave.

Everyone was getting ready to leave the ship. The Captain shook everyone's hand as each person left. It was his final voyage on the Great Lakes. He won over the hearts of every passenger on this trip. Everyone wished him well when he sailed the high seas.

People who knew each other before the voyage seemed cheerier and closer. People who had just met on this adventure left feeling like old friends.

I knew deep down that it was just a cruise with a nice companion. I had the time of my life and to ask for anything more would be selfish.

It was my turn to shake hands with the Captain and I expressed my thanks for the lighthearted tone he set for this cruise.

As I got off the ship, I looked for my bags, spotted them and then I looked for my mother.

I saw our car and my mom had just stepped out and was looking around.

I ran up to her and put my arms around her.

"Did you have a good time?"

"I couldn't have dreamed up a better trip. It was wonderful."

I got my bags and loaded them in the car. Then, once I got in, Kat said that she got my postcard.

"You made the Thomas Edison Inn sound so quaint that I think we should stop by and see it since we are already here. It's not too far away from here, is it?

"No, it's not far at all. That's a great idea. I'm not ready to end my vacation yet."

I told my mom she could park the car and we could walk to the inn because it is so pretty along the river. I looked up and the sun was shining.

"Forget it. I'm in heels. Let's drive." Kat put the car in motion and we passed the charming café where James and I had stopped before. People were eating outside and looking at a gorgeous view. We went inside the inn and it took a minute or two for our eyes to adjust to the dim lighting inside.

Kat and I entered the lobby with no firm game plan.

"Let's eat lunch here," Kat said.

It sounded good to me. The host took us in the dining room and to a table with a great view. As my mother was taking in the ambience I looked behind me and saw a smaller room to the side. I hadn't noticed that room during my first visit to the inn.

I asked Kat why the inn would have two dining rooms. She said that it's probably for private parties. It sounded as if a party was in progress.

I was glad that someone was having a good time. Just because I had my first less-than-perfect day in this week of wonders didn't mean that other people had to stop enjoying themselves. My disappointed mood was improving.

I heard more laughter. I thought it sounded familiar but I was so busy feeling sorry for myself that my observational skills were lacking. Still, I swore I knew that laugh.

The waiter brought us menus and Kat wanted a minute to decide her choice. I already knew what I wanted...soup...no salad...no both. Okay, so I needed a minute also.

I forgot about the other dining room until I heard another laugh, different from the first and yet still familiar to me.

I looked at Kat.

"Mom?"

"Yes?"

"I can't stand it. I've got to see who is in the private dining room. Will you come with me?"

"Do I have a choice?"

We edged over to the room and peeked in. I just saw the backs of two men...one gent looked on in years while the other guy looked to be about my age. I noticed a pile of photos spread out on one of the tables.

I was about to forget the whole thing when Uncle Ned looked up!

"Bea!"

"Uncle Ned! What are you doing here? And by the way, thank you a so much for this incredible trip!" I ran toward him. As I did, I noticed that he was sitting with James.

"James?" I mumbled, looking dumbfounded.

Uncle Ned spoke up before James could. "Your buddy here called me ship-to-shore saying that he had to meet the character in all the stories you told on board. James also wanted to thank me for sending you on this trip. He wanted to surprise you. He really likes you kid."

James just looked up and grinned.

Kat came over and introduced herself to James. "So, you're the James I've heard so much about."

James replied, "After this trip I feel as if I know all of Bea's family. May I call you Kat?"

"I'd look out for this one, Kat. He's a charmer," Ned said. "Kat, come over here and look at these pictures."

Kat and I walked over and saw artwork on film. James captured not only the images but also the spirit of the Great Lakes. When I looked at his photographs I sensed nature's majesty.

"You can tell James gets the essence of his subject matter." I said that as I held up a picture of me with my nose all scrunched up.

"No Bea," Ned said. "This picture tells the real story."

It was a photo of James and me on the deck, looking out at the vast blue horizon. His arms were wrapped around me and the wind was blowing my hair in all directions. We both faced forward as if we were both of the same mindset. We were both smiling. No doubt James had just told one of his corny jokes.

"Where did you get this?" I wondered.

"The ship's photographer took it," James responded.

"May I keep it?"

"Of course. I made a copy for me too."

"I hate to ruin a perfect moment but does this mean that I might see you again?" I asked James quietly.

"See him again? For God's sake Bea, he set up this whole reunion!" Ned stated.

"When you just waved goodbye without saying a word, I was crushed. It surprised me because the time I spent with you made me feel as if I was the most important person in the world."

"Oh, I definitely think you are important." He came over and gave me a hug.

"Bea," Kat said. "James has a gift. He sees beauty in places that the rest of us overlook. That makes him unique."

"Oh he's more than unique. He's rare and wonderful," I whispered. "James," I continued. "I've liked you from the time we first met at the hotel. The more I got to know you, the better my vacation became. You made what would have been a fun trip into the best vacation of my life. It was perfect. Thank you!" I felt a warm trickle run down my cheek.

"Don't forget the person who is responsible for us meeting in the first place." James looked at my Uncle Ned.

I went over and gave Ned a hug. "How did you know that I would have such a magical voyage?"

"I've always told you that all of that fresh water in one place, here in the Great Lakes, is mystical." Ned patted me on the back as he spoke. "Besides, I don't deserve all the credit. James did some swift maneuvering to get this whole meeting to work out."

Before I could say anything else, James spoke up. "Our trip might be over but our journey has just begun."